CW01512815

FEMINIZED AND PRETTY

3

Turned into a submissive sexy girl by his vengeful wife

(Femdom and Transgender Series, Book 3)

Lady Alexa

This novel is a work of fiction. Names, characters, businesses, places, events and incidents are either the products of the author's imagination or used in a fictitious manner. Any resemblance to actual persons, living or dead, or actual events is purely coincidental.

Contains explicit scenes of a sexual nature including forced male to female gender transformation, female domination, humiliation, CFNM, spanking and reluctant feminisation. All characters in this story are aged 18 and over.

Strictly for adults aged 18 and over.

You can follow my female led relationship and forced feminization blog at:

___www.ladyalexauk.com___

You can also subscribe to my newsletter from this site and receive FLR and Forced feminisation news and other offers.

*Contact me regarding this or any other of my books at **___ladyalexa@mail.com___**.*
I love to hear from my readers

CONTENTS

For this third and final book in the series, I've switched the point of view of the story, from the third person perspective of the previous two books, to the first person.

I did this so I can describe more fully the feelings and emotions Patrick / Patricia experiences in the ultimate stages of his forced-feminisation at the hands of his vengeful wife Elizabeth.

I'd appreciate it if you could leave a book review for me..

Chapter 1 - New Boobs

I held my flared cotton skirt down against the soft breeze. I strode home towards the station after my first day back at work. I didn't want the bulge in my panties to give away my hidden reality. I fought the feelings in my stomach as the light cotton flapped against the top of my bare legs in the open air.

I pulled my panties up as tightly as possible into my crotch. It was an attempt to flatten the masculine bulge threatening to peek below my tiny cotton wisp of a skirt. A small gust of wind or a moment of excitement would expose the facts: I was a man forced to dress like a woman. My scanty female clothing kept me in a constant state of excitement.

The early evening sun threw long shadows across the pavement. I was pleased to have completed my first day back working in the pub with few incidents. The trouble was that my home gave me little respite from my torture.

The summer warmth touched my smooth bare legs. It gave me new sensations and new experiences: all were pleasurable and arousing. My long full-bodied platinum-blond hair bounced against my back like slow waves against the beach. It had grown long and flowed halfway down my back. I found it reassuring and sexy. A new person stirred inside me, a female overpowering my old male self.

I puffed in short breaths. I had no room to take deeper breaths; a corset shaped my waist down to 24 inches. I didn't think I would be able to move or breathe when my wife Elizabeth had first pulled it on me. I became used to it over the day. It helped me to look as good as I did — I was determined to live with it.

It had been my first day back at work as a waitress in the gastropub owned by my nemesis, Fiona Allerton. It had been my first day back at work after recovering from the operation. The operation made me look as good as I now did. It also caused a stir with the male clientele.

The weight of my new boobs would take some getting used to. They were much bigger than I'd expected them to be. I was getting used to standing and walking upright under their weight. They were out of proportion to me slim body but Elizabeth had wanted them for me.

I leant back to find the new equilibrium in

my body. My chest bounced about like two over-inflated water-filled balloons. My low-cut bra and top pushed my new tits up giving them maximum exposure. A deep mountainous cleavage remained in my vision. The view caused a permanent tingle of excitement in my penis.

Lecherous stares accompanied each step of my walk to the station and every bounce of my enormous breasts. It was fifteen minutes of being the centre of attention for every male in the area. Their eyes burned into my two mountains. Piercing glares from women bounced off me like pellets on armour plating.

My stomach tingled and my head felt light at the admiration and adoration of my looks. They were from men which was humiliating. Women stared with hostility. I liked to think it was because I looked better than most of them. They were jealous.

Excitement bubbled in my stomach at my new exaggerated feminine appearance. I was sexy and when I was a struggling male musician I would have been the type I'd have gone for. Yet, at the same time, the humiliation ate into my every thought. I didn't know what to think. I'd become a male's female fantasy and I was overjoyed and sexually excited by this. I despised myself for the enjoyment.

This tornado of contradictions swirled inside me. How can something be so liberating and awful at the same time? I could find no answer to this conundrum.

I turned the corner into the street where I lived. I thought about my surrender to my wife's insistence I have breast implants. I was always going to lose that debate; I had little say in how I looked these days. Now I looked like a girl, she had softened her attitude towards me. A little. She treated me more kindly and I wanted more of her kindness.

I hadn't wanted an operation to give me female breasts. I understood her point about me having real breasts. Her argument was clear and it was logical, it always was. It started with her statement my feminisation was not negotiable and I had to look like a girl. That was a fact I had to accept.

She'd explained it was an act of kindness to give me real women's breasts, they would help me to blend in as a girl. They would remove some of the humiliation I was feeling. Perhaps she cared after all. I'm not sure that was the reason.

My old false breast forms did not look the part, they were not real. My not-so-loving wife, Elizabeth, had told me the residual areas of my former masculinity, would be less obvious when I had real female breasts.

She couldn't do much about my wide shoulders and fascial structure and I saw her argument. It made sense. I wanted to be able to return to being a man, but this was not permitted. Instead, I had received something to help me to blend in as a female. It was an act of kindness by my wife. That's what she told me.

The private doctor doing the operation had been clear. I had to request and sign I wanted to look like a woman and to have the new breasts. I signed, what else could I do? I confess there was a frisson of excitement at Elizabeth pushing me into the decision. It was out of my hands, not my decision. She had coerced and forced me. I was not guilty of wanting to look more like a woman.

I did make one mistake. I hadn't discussed my proposed breast size with my wife. She had said my new breasts would be appropriate for me and I had assumed appropriate meant discreet. It hadn't. She tricked me. In Elizabeth's mind, appropriate meant breasts that matched the look she had in mind for me. It was my fault for not checking, not being clear.

With my enormous shock of blond hair, tiny skirts and towering heels, she said I needed 42DD breasts to match. This was what I now had. I looked like a provocative exaggerated girl.

Some might say I looked like a living Barbie Doll.

Chapter 2 - Long legs and blond hair

I pushed away my thoughts on the recent past and the enormous changes I'd gone through. My six-inch heels clipped on the pavement like a trotting pony on cobblestones.

I'd become proficient walking in high heels. My calf muscles were shorter and my foot tendons longer. I walked on tiptoes in these sandals but it gave me with no problem any more. It made me take shorter steps, to be more feminine. I supposed this was my wife's plan.

I admired my new look in mirrors and shop windows as I made my way down the hill towards the station. I wanted to check all was fine, nothing more. I'd done that when I was a man, I'd been a good-looking man. Now I was good looking as a woman.

I reached the station and passed to the ticket barrier. I flicked my travelcard against the reader and the barriers swung open with a clatter. My long pink nails contrasted against the blue card as I hurried through. I put the travelcard back in my small pink leather handbag and pulled the shoulder strap over my head. I didn't want it snatched on the underground train. I was a vulnerable girl with vertiginous high heels and a chest unsuitable for running after a thief.

I found a seat, looked down at my hands, slim but wide. They were a man's hands. Some things were beyond the reach of my wife. I settled down for the ride, my legs closed at the knees to hide my skimpy underwear. The unfeminine bulge inside them was semi-hard thanks to the clothes.

The train clattered on the tracks as it picked up speed. I peered through the blond fringe over my eyes. A middle-aged man stared back. His bulging paunch burst against the buttons of a cheap white shirt. The button holes stretched and pasty white skin peeked through.

His eyes flicked across my sleek hairless legs and tumbling cleavage. The soft material of my skirt lay across the top of my thighs like a small white ribbon. My legs were no longer the legs of any man I had ever known. Were these shapely limbs mine and not some sexy girl's? I sat up straighter and ran a hand over my thigh. I didn't want a man ogling me but it proved what I thought. My legs were damn good.

What was not good was having to work at

Fiona's gastropub as a waitress. Manual work was not my thing and waitressing was worse. Actually, work was not my thing. I'd had to endure the comments and occasional gropes from the male customers.

Elizabeth had turned me into a bimbo girl as a punishment but working as a waitress was my real punishment. This humiliation had become worse today thanks to my new oversized tits. The customers already looked at me as if their eyes were on springs. Now their eyes fed on my breasts like suckling babies.

The more polite and friendly male customers told me I was pretty. They flirted not realising what I was underneath. Or maybe they knew. My skirt was so short I'm sure they got an eyeful an times. At least their compliments validated my appearance and who doesn't enjoy compliments? It wasn't so nice to be told you're pretty by a man. Or was it?

The train pulled into my home station. I got out of the carriage and left the station. I walked to the high street and to my wife's home. It certainly wasn't my home; it was the house I lived in. The sun shone over the roofs. The trees lined the street like swaying silent soldiers in tall green bearskin hats. Beams of sunlight flickered through the thick leaves and danced around my feet like tiny fairies.

The breeze had dropped and it was a warm evening. It was an amazing feeling to be outside with bare legs and a short skirt. Refreshing air swirled and settled around the tops of my thighs and crotch in a way trousers and shorts could never allow. I pushed the thought away, shocked at my abject surrender to Elizabeth's version of my new femininity.

The walk home passed without any unusual incidents. I endured the stares and the van drivers who hooted their horns at me. My long bare legs, straining breasts, short skirt and platinum blonde hair attracted attention.

I reached the house where I lived with my wife. It was wide and Edwardian with a black and white tiled front path. I walked up the path and entered my front door. My cheeks steamed hot from the exertion of the walk and the attention I'd attracted. I closed the door to the background sound of droning traffic and a bird cawing.

There was no sound inside, it was as if the

house were deserted. A faint floral smell drifted through. I tried to remove my shoes but I'd forgotten the tiny padlocks on my six-inch heels. Another of Elizabeth's amusing innovations. It was probably for the best. Walking barefooted would have been uncomfortable now my tendons had contracted to match my new raised foot positions.

I stayed by the front door for a moment to wind down and take in my first day out after the breast operation. My hair had grown longer during my recovery and fell down my back in huge swirling blond waves. A pretty stylist had put a wavy style in it yesterday. My figure was shaped by a low-fat low-carbohydrate diet and the restricting corset. My entire physical appearance had changed. Not even my late parents would have recognised me now.

Something else had changed and I wasn't resentful. I enjoyed the looks and loved the attention. I swooned at sensation of my soft skirt against my smooth thighs. The tautness of my calves in six-inch heels was exciting. My hair swirled around my face and fell over my bare shoulders. These were new and exciting sensations. Something stirred in my panties.

I stared at myself in the hall mirror. My wife was shifting my masculinity away like flour through a sieve. I liked it.

Chapter 3 - The cuckold event

"Is that you, Patty?" Elizabeth's voice boomed out from the living room. I tore my attention away from the hall mirror. M eyes wanted to cling to my feminine face for a few more moments. My permanent make-up almost disguised a square masculine facial structure.

I answered, "Yes, Ms Remington."

Calling my wife by her title and surname never failed to rankle me. I had little choice. I had no other home, no friends, no family and no money. She had me by the balls, metaphorically and often physically.

"Come in here now, girl."

She sounded terse, not a great sign. Elizabeth's more gentle approach of the past few weeks appeared to have dissipated. I trundled into the living room expecting the worst.

My fears were confirmed. Fiona Allerton sat in an armchair opposite my less-than-adoring wife. Fiona Allerton, my tormentor and my wife's advisor on my spiralling feminisation.

Worse still, my wife's lover Dan Hunter stood by the bay window. He had one hand in a pocket as if imitating a smooth film star of the fifties. His clipped silver hair was immaculately parted on one side. The creases in the trousers of his light-grey suit were as sharp as hunting-knife blades. His shoes sparkled gloss black. A shaft of sunlight from the window glinted on his crooked smile. His brilliant white teeth must have been the result of hours in an orthodontist's surgery. They dazzled like pure snow under an arctic sun.

"Wow, Elizabeth. If you hadn't told me it was your husband, I would have thought it was a real girl." Dan Hunter folded his arms and nodded in approval. I shuddered at the glint of lust in his eyes as they fell on my cleavage. It was the first time he'd seen me with my new tits.

I curtsied to my wife Elizabeth and then to Fiona. Elizabeth's face dropped, thunderous. "And Mr Hunter?"

I bit hard and clenched my jaw. I heard it creak. It was bad enough being subservient to women, but to be submissive to this smarmy man was banging my wife. Elizabeth's slap was unexpected and her palm stung against my cheek. It was a reminder I had to curtsey to this man. It was out of my hands. I bared my teeth in hate as I dropped my knee and turned my eyes to the floor. I performed the curtsey towards Dan Hunter's general direction. The best rebellion I could get away with as my fingers held my little skirt out and my face burnt like hot coals.

"Better." Elizabeth's stern response was cool. I didn't like this atmosphere it spelt trouble.

Fiona Allerton cleared her throat and beckoned me towards her. "Remove your skirt, top and panties, Patty. I want to talk about the next stage of your feminisation."

Straight to the point. Fiona Allerton was an expert in enforced male feminisation and Elizabeth had employed her to manage my feminisation.

I looked towards Elizabeth who stared back without emotion. Dan Hunter's smile widened further. I hadn't thought that possible. I closed my eyes, I wanted to disappear. I wanted things to remain as they were now. I'd gone a long way and accepted my femininity. Why did they have to change things again? It was true my boobs were far too big and uncomfortable but at least I got attention. The room fell into silence.

My arms moved like lead, I didn't want to follow Fiona's instruction. I felt Dan's eyes burn into me.

I pushed down my skirt and let it drop to my ankles. I pulled my tight top over my head like stripping away the peel from a piece of fruit. My breasts bounced, held in by my straining bra. I slipped down my panties and balanced on one leg. My penis sprung free, it was erect and firm. My cotton panties snagged on one of my stiletto heels. I cursed under my breath as I staggered and swayed on my heels like a drunken flamingo.

Elizabeth sighed at my awkward self-consciousness. I pulled my panties off the long heel. I had to do what she told me. It was best to avoid the punishment. I laid my clothing at my feet and stood in my corset, restraining bra and the six-inch heels. My hands hovered over my erection.

"Hands by your side," Elizabeth snapped.

I flung them to my side. Elizabeth twisted a key on a chain around her neck. The key to the two small padlocks around my ankles locking my shoes on.

Fiona moved in and slid onto her haunches to study my penis and balls. She pressed with two chilly fingers, pushing my penis to one side then the other. A serious look was etched into her stern school-mistress face. Her dark straight hair was pulled back from her face. She'd tied it into a bun at the back of her head.

Her black pencil skirt trained tight against fine black tights and firm thighs. She peered over the top of dark-framed glasses perched on the end of a long Roman nose. She rubbed my smooth hairless testicles between her fingertips. Her red lips pursed in concentration, her grey shadowed eyes slitted in concentration.

She pushed my balls to one side then the other. She made humming noises as she inspected me. She ran a finger down my penis, across the tattoo that said *clitty,* and along the top. Elizabeth smirked.

Fiona slid her hands up and down my corseted waist above my hips. She ran a finger over the other humiliating tattoo on my stomach: *This slut is the property of Elizabeth Remington.* She nodded at my erection, pulsing and throbbing with desperation.

"Elizabeth, this is the proof of what we need to do."

A tug of apprehension and dread greeted her words. I had already undergone breast surgery and permanent make-up tattooed onto my face. I was marked as a female for life. I had a Latina flick tattooed at the outer corner of my eyes and permanent smokey-grey lids with thin arched tattooed eyebrows. My face was feminine. What more could they do to me?

"You need to consider the reconstruction of Patty's penis and balls into a vagina," Fiona said.

I gulped. My stomach fell and turned. Fiona

had talked about this before but I never considered my wife would go that far. A wave of panic hit me and I went to pull away and run. I flapped my hands. Fiona was talking about operating on my penis, this was a step too far. I'd agreed to the breasts but I'd never allow them to remove the final vestige of my manhood. I looked across at Elizabeth, my pleading look was met with a stony glare.

Fiona continued. "This little thing serves no purpose any more, especially as you have a real man to give you what you need, Elizabeth."

Fiona pulled my penis about like she was steering a video game joystick. My stick wasn't feeling so joyful. It was rock hard though.

"I have some ideas about what to do with this little pathetic thing." Fiona flicked my penis again dismissively. A look of disgust pulled across her face.

I should have become used to this but I hadn't. Who could get used to having their once private parts exposed and humiliated? I vowed to myself they would never do what they threatened.

"You can see why I needed a real man like Dan. Patty's little clitty is no use to anyone." Elizabeth looked at Dan, her face softened as their eyes locked.

I stood horrified and beyond embarrassment. Dan chuckled through his fingers from the other side of the room. He appeared comfortable watching events and seemed to find it amusing.

Fiona's face hardened. "Elizabeth, I'm serious about this. You should think about having her little sissy stick and pussy balls removed. A plastic surgeon can re-sculpture them into a vagina. Now Patty is a girl, it makes sense. There's going back."

I stepped back and my penis dropped from Fiona's fingers. I gasped for breath. My heartbeat gathered pace as if I was speeding downhill. I couldn't stop them. My heart banged against the wall of my chest like a jack-hammer. I'd gone a long way down the feminine path: this was too far.

"Or...," Fiona said.

I looked up hoping, for some respite.

"The other option is you retain Patty's clitty and pussy balls but ensure she is regularly milked. This way we remove any nasty male urges."

As if to prove her point my erection was pointing at her. It had been a while since I had cum. Despite, or maybe because of, Fiona's manner I was excited by her attention on my penis.

"We can also tuck her — push her pussy balls into her body and tape up her little clitty."

They were discussing my most intimate parts as if I wasn't there. I was a piece of meat to do with as they wanted.

Elizabeth put a finger to her chin. "I'll take the second option for now. Adding breasts was a major improvement but it's a big step to remove bits of her. I'll need to think about it. Besides, I like the tattoo on her little penis saying clitty. It's funny."

I sighed a long blow of relief. I wasn't sure

what milking meant but I felt as if I'd won a reprieve.

Fiona nodded in agreement, her face etched hard. "I understand, Elizabeth, but we have a problem while the clitty and pussy balls are still there. For Patty's next stage of feminisation, we will be reducing the length of her skirts and dresses even further. Any hint of a bulge in her panties will spoil the look as it would hang below the hem. We have to ensure her crotch area is flat and feminine since it will be on show."

I swallowed hard as Fiona and Elizabeth mirrored each other's expressions. They were locked in sync. My skirts were already micro length, they hardly covered my panties. They were level with the bottom of my panties. *How much shorter could they be?*

Chapter 4 - Micro skirts

Dan moved away from the window and sauntered to the bookcase. He took out a heavy hardback and flicked through it. The title read *Organisational Development*. How typical of Elizabeth to have business books on her shelves. She had little time for novels, everything was business for her, including dealing with me. I still didn't know what Dan did for a living. His suit and the gold Rolex told me it was well-paid work.

Fiona pulled me towards her by my erect penis. She let go and fished around in a wide black leather bag on the floor. She pulled out latex gloves and slapped them on like a doctor about to operate. I wanted to back away. This didn't look good.

The slap of the gloves caught Dan's attention and he glanced up from his book. A single groomed eyebrow arched. Why were there no white hairs in his brows to match his steel-coloured hair? Steel, was that even a natural shade? Fiona pushed my head down until I was bent over and looking at the floor. My bare bum faced my wife. Fiona passed me a tissue.

"Hold this around your clitty, sissy girl."

Blood rushed to my head and I did what she ordered, cupping the paper tissue around my erection. To my horror, Dan was watching every moment with rapt attention. Fiona called out for my wife's personal assistant, Clara, to join us. Clara entered moments later, wide black trousers flapping around her ankles. I'd never seen Clara in a dress. Her muscular shoulders reminded me of a swimmer's figure. Her straight fair hair was pulled back in a tight ponytail. It swung from side to side as she walked.

Cold gel slap onto my bare bum cheeks before Fiona pushed a finger into my rectum. I jerked up with the shock and the chill of the gel.

"Ladies, and gentleman, watch carefully. I'm going to show you how to milk pretty Patty. She needs to be cleaned out at least three times a day to remove her residual male urges."

Fiona removed a long plastic drumstick-like device from her bag. She smeared a clear gel along its length and pushed it on mu bum hole. I felt the cold pressure against my anus. The drumstick slipped inside me. I tried to straighten instinctively; a hand on the back of my head pushed me back down. T

A wave of odd pleasure washed over me. Fiona twisted the stick further inside me. It touched something and orgasmic pangs spread through me. An orgasm built as she continued to press the stick device inside me. I erupted into the tissue with a force I'd never experienced before. If this was milking, I wanted more.

A slow clap sounded from the other side of the room. It was Dan. My moment of pleasure blew away like a feather in a gale.

"Wash your mess down the toilet and then come back, Patty, I haven't finished with you." Fiona stood up.

I straightened up, holding the tissue of cum. I ran to the toilet, my huge boobs bounced and strained against the tight bra. I flushed the sticky tissue away and washed the strings of gooey discharge from between my fingers. I crept back into the silent waiting living room.

Fiona called me to her with a wiggle of her index finger. I stood before her, my breasts blocked my view of my shrivelled penis. Fiona had everyone's attention.

"Patty's become too used to mini skirts and high heels. She enjoys wearing them and we don't want her enjoying that, do we? Her appearance attracts male customers into my gastropub. I'd like to improve her look further. To make her look more slutty."

I froze at her words. Fiona rooted around in her holdall bag and produced a piece of stretchy white material and a bra.

"For the next stage, I want to reduce the

length of Patty's skirts further."

Was she serious? They barely covered my bum cheeks and panties. Fiona held up the white Lycra material. It was no more than a four-inch wide elastic belt. She told me to put it on. I took it and looked it over. I slipped it over my feet and pulled the tiny skirt up. The hem was level with the base of my penis, covering my pubic triangle but not my penis and balls. I was fully exposed. I looked down behind me. My bum cheeks were visible. This wasn't decent, they couldn't expect to me go out like this. The skirt covered nothing.

Fiona produced another tiny skirt from her bag, it was bright red with thin pencil pleats. She told me to remove the tight white skirt and try this one on. It was the same length, four inches and covered nothing. My limp penis hung below the hem, my bum cheeks showed. The skirt was little more than a decoration around my hips. I had to say something, I'd be arrested for indecent exposure.

"Mistress Allerton, I can't wear this, I would get into trouble."

Fiona sneered at me. "I hope so. You will be wearing these skirts outside the house from now on. You're going to get a lot of male admirers dressed like this."

Eyes turned to Elizabeth.

"I want her to go out dressed like this," she squealed with excitement.

Pressure built up in my chest as I thought about having to go out and work in a four-inch long skirt. My breathing became faster, I thought I might faint. "But, Ms Remington, my clitty will show."

"Your clitty won't show, Patty," said Fiona. "I have a solution for that." Fiona pulled me back towards her by my limp penis. "Watch this, ladies and gentleman. We call this the tuck. I'm going to put Patty's nasty pussy balls inside her. It's where they go when it's cold."

With a twist, she popped my balls inside me. I lifted what there was of my pleated skirt. My stomach twisted. All I saw was a single limp penis, shrivelled with my loose foreskin rumpled like a screwed-up cloth. My balls were gone, tucked inside me. It looked weird. A dark cloud fell over my eyes. I swayed. I thought I might faint.

Fiona took a length of wide silver tape and stuck one end to my stomach above my pubic hair triangle. She wound it over my penis and up over my bum behind and pulled it tight. She then gave me a pair of white panties. They had a small rubber mould shape fitted inside.

Fiona lifted it out and turned it over. "It's a rubber mould in the shape of a vagina." She held the panties up in the air and waved them around for Elisabeth and Dan to see. "Under Patty's panties, it will look as if she has a vagina. They are for transvestites or transgenders before their op. The lips will be outlined through the tight material of her panties."

Elizabeth shrieked. "Fiona, you're a genius."

She placed the vagina mould back into my panties and I pulled them up. I gasped. The lips of a vagina were outlined. I dropped the hem of my skirt. Skirt? It didn't qualify for that name, a frilly belt was a better description.

Fiona positioned me in front of a full-length mirror. I put a hand to my mouth; I was unable to stop a shriek. The contours of my fake vagina lips showed against the cotton below the hem of the skirt. My panties were on full view. Fiona twisted me around. The bottom of my bum cheeks showed. The thin line of my g-string was hidden inside the crack of my bottom cheeks. She had artfully twisted the tape into a string under my g-string.

"You'll be wearing these tiny skirts from now on. You'll travel to work and back working in them at my pub." She sniffed. "Your panties will cover you so there's no exposure and you won't be arrested."

I wanted to be sick. I couldn't even feel my

penis, it had gone to sleep with the tightness of the tape. So this was how a girl felt. No penis. No balls.

Fiona stood in front of me. "But we haven't finished yet. Patty, remove your bra."

Dan put his book on the table and folded his arms. I had his full leering attention as I removed my bra. My breasts flopped out with unrestrained relief. They protruded like two giant bombs. Dan's eyes were on stalks at seeing my exposed 42DD boobs. Fiona passed me a thin bra. This wouldn't fit me, surely? The cups weren't big enough, they seemed to be only the lower half of a bra cup.

I pulled the bra on and did it up at the front. I twisted it around my chest. I tried to pull it over my nipples. It fitted under my breasts, lifting them. The cup fitted under my breast and my nipples showed, firm and erect.

Fiona passed me a white tee-shirt. It was too small for me and had a deep, wide-open front. I pulled it over my head, body and corset. It squeezed against my body. I untucked my hair from the neckline and shook my head. The top fitted like a tight latex glove around my slim body and my enormous boobs. My nipples stuck out like two angry bee stings beneath the thin tight cotton.

"I want the men to see the shape of your nipples through your top and the old bras didn't do that. This is far better." Fiona stifled a chuckle.

The top hugged my breasts leaving nothing to the imagination. The bra pulled my chest together giving a deep valley of cleavage. My nipples had become more sensitive since my enlargement surgery and were erect. A sliver of my areola peeked out around the exposed area of my new low top. My mouth dropped.

I looked down at my new clothing, what there was of it. This was a joke. Surely Elizabeth wouldn't make me leave the house dressed like this? They had to be teasing, right?

Chapter 5 -Feminized and exposed

I stood still in the storeroom of the gastropub, balanced on six-inch heels. My panties were loose around my ankles and I held my knees together. I had my fist around my rock-hard penis. My skin-tight pencil skirt scrunched up above my pubic triangle. My balls were missing, pushed up into my body.

Suzie, the gastropub manager, giggled. She had made me show her where Elizabeth had tucked them in that morning. My face still burned from her inspection and from poking them with one of her short red nails.

The metal shelves around me were stacked with jars of mayonnaise and tomato ketchup. Suzie stood back on the other side of the room facing me. She struggled to contain her giggles. Her hands lay on her broad hips while she tapped a foot on the floor.

She was a plain lady of around forty. A grey line along the top of her head showed where her dyed blond hair roots needed to be touched up. Dark eyebrows gave away her true hair colour. Dark-blue trousers strained against wide hips and large bum. I guessed she had put on some weight since she'd bought these clothes.

Fiona had asked Suzie to oversee my milking before starting work. Clara had milked me before I left home with the plastic drumstick up my bottom. I had to masturbate with Suzie glaring at me with growing impatience and intermittent giggles. I managed an erection; that surprised me. I found nothing about Suzie or the location exciting. Or so I thought.

Suzie's amused stare and tapping foot told me I needed to hurry up. If I was in doubt she added, "Hurry up, stupid, I've got a pub to run."

I pumped my hand along my shaft and a warm glow ran down my erection. Something about her off-hand manner was exciting. I orgasmed. The first couple of spasms were dry but then a thin trickle oozed into the tissue I held over the end. My discharge was pathetic, Fiona's regime was working. I was being bled dry of any sexual desire.

Suzie's face dropped and her smile faded. She looked to the ceiling in disgust as I cleaned up and stuck the tape back over my limp penis. I pulled my panties up and attempted to pull my skirt hem down. It was futile, it was far too short to cover the bottom half of my panties or my bum cheeks. I was about to start work with my breasts tumbling out, my bum showing and the contour of the fake vagina lips visible below the front of my skirt.

The journey to work had been the worst of my entire forced-feminisation experience. Elizabeth and Fiona had not been teasing. Cheers and vans hooting had greeted me from the moment I left the house. I'd heard whispered words of, "*disgusting*"and "*prostitute*." I'd endured the leers on the train. I'd had to position my handbag over my crotch area as my skirt rose high above my panties. I might as well have gone out in just the panties.

Elizabeth had won again. I'd begun to enjoy the feeling of Elizabeth feminising me and she couldn't stand that. She wanted me in discomfort, she wanted me humiliated and unhappy. I yearned for the comfort of mid-thigh light skirts flowing around my smooth legs.

When I used to play the guitar in bars, the audience were more interested in drinking, chatting and laughing. I was the background sound to their evening out. No one noticed me back when I was a male, except the young girls who wanted a bohemian man. They lost interest when they found I had no money. Now I had everyone's attention. Now I looked like a bimbo.

I'd made a mistake letting Elizabeth see I enjoyed my new femininity. The permanent make-up and long hair she had given me had become something to be enjoyed. Instead of fighting it, I'd embraced it. That had not been in

Elizabeth's plan, she wanted me to suffer. I was paying the cost of my stupidity. I should have pretended to fight it, to pretend to hate it. Instead, I'd preened in the mirrors. Elizabeth had seen her feminisation punishment failing. I should have known she would react. How could I have been so stupid? So vain.

I was open to ridicule. I was going to be serving in a bar with everything on show.

Suzie and I left the storeroom and returned to the bar area. I watched Suzie unbolt the front doors of the gastropub with a heavy trepidation in my chest. Soon the customers would soon be streaming in for lunch. This was a place popular with the office workers of the area, mainly a male clientele.

My stomach did cartwheels as Suzie walked

back to the bar swinging her wide hips. She threw me a lop-sided grin as she passed, her eyes flicked to my false vagina. Her smile widened.

The front door swung open and three young men strolled in. They chatted and laughed together and found a table on the far side of the pub. They sat down still chatting. They hadn't noticed me, too caught up on their amusing discussion. I heard them discussing goals, football players, the Premier League. They opened the laminated menus propped up between the sauce bottles.

I waited by the bar with Cristina, the other waitress. Cristina was a young Romanian girl who looked at me with undisguised contempt.

Suzie's lips brushed against my ear. "Go and

ask the nice gentlemen if they'd like a drink before they choose their food, Patty."

My stomach formed a knot. My intestines twisted and tightened. I swallowed hard. Her plain face stared back. She brushed a lock of hair away from her eye and tucked it behind an ear. I hesitated a moment, still hidden behind the wooden bar of the pub. Suzie made a waving motion with her hand. I was being ushered to serve the men at the table.

I tottered out from behind the bar. The little padlocks tapped against my ankle buckles like a little warning bell. I looked across at the customers, chatting and reading their menus. I tugged at my skirt. The false vagina rubbed between my leg tops. Pulling on my skirt wasn't going to lengthen it. I checked I'd pulled the tape tight enough to flatten my penis. The clear shape of my false vagina lips showed through my tight panties below the hem of my tiny white pencil skirt. The skirt covered only the top of my panties. It was like a second skin. I looked back at Suzie a final time. She ushered me away towards the men.

I had a new problem. My top was so open it exposed the areola around my nipples and my nipple was almost popping out. I pulled my top with two manicured fingers but it flicked back. My erect nipples showed through my top anyway but I didn't want them exposed entirely.

I walked towards the table, my head down, imitating someone relaxed while a turmoil wound itself around inside me. My legs turned to jelly. I was going to have to accept this as the latest extreme humiliation in my life. I stopped beside the three male customers. I tried to say something but the words caught in my dry throat. They hadn't looked up. I pulled at my skirt hem as I wiggled my hips. I cleared my throat. I told myself to use a high female voice.

"Can I get you a drink, gentlemen, while you choose your food?" My voice wobbled and came out higher than intended. Like a cartoon character on helium.

The man nearest me looked up and then back to his menu. His brain took a few instants to register what he'd seen. He looked up again in slow motion as his mouth opened. My legs shook like jelly in a washing machine on full spin. The man's eyes widened. They feasted over my breasts. His eyes fell to my crotch. They fixed onto my artificial vagina lips, showing beneath the skirt hem. My white panties were taut against the false vagina lips. I felt sick at the lust glistening in the man's eyes. He licked his lips. A man. Lusting after me?

His companions looked at him and then to me. Two more mouths dropped open. It was like watching three chicks waiting to be fed. I pushed my knees together to try to hide my false vagina outline. I was hunching. The scene must have looked bizarre as Suzie came over,

"Stand up straight, girl," she barked.

I shot up straight, like a soldier on guard. It was too much for one of my straining breasts and an erect nipple popped out. I shoved it back after a short moment of shock. I was too late, they had seen it. Suzie sniggered and the men gaped.

Tears welled in my eyes, my throat locked. I moved to run but Suzie's icy stare held me there. I wobbled on my stilt-like heels, my head swimming and nauseous. How could I live and work like this?

The three men stared at me, soaking up my body, absorbing me like dry sponges. Still unable to tear their eyes away, one of them ordered three soft drinks. Suzie ushered me away to get the drinks with a contemptuous flick of the hand. I picked the drinks up at the bar from Micaela, the bar girl who eyed me up and down like a piece of dirt on her shoe. She swapped glances with Cristina.

I stopped at the bar, trying to compose myself, my back to the dining area. A cool breeze from an open window flowed around my bare exposed bum. My boobs strained against my top, my nipples stood erect and firm. The disconcerting feeling of having no penis or balls made me nauseous all over again.

Behind me, the dining area was filling up with customers. I had to keep moving or Suzie would be onto me again. I took the drinks to the table and bent over to place them in front of the three young men. They ogled my cleavage with unconcealed lust. Suzie watched me, one side of her lip and a cheek curled up.

"Now serve the other customers, there's a good girl." Suzie folded her arms.

Blood rushed into my cheeks, anger and humiliation hit me in equal measures. This was my most difficult time so far. I'd struggled to accept my feminisation at my wife's hands then I embraced it. This was too far. Elizabeth and Fiona had turned me into an exhibitionist bimbo.

I turned to the next table to serve another customer. My eyes closed in despair. Drops of sweat beaded on my cheeks despite the coolness of the day. I tried to open my eyes, but it was as if my lids were locked. I wanted to hide as the sound of voices increased in the pub. I wanted to pretend I was somewhere else. I imagined myself again as a man, playing my guitar in a bar.

Instead, I was thinking about the next humiliation I was about to face? Who would be leering at me next?

Chapter 6 – A feminized fate

I forced my eyes open. It wasn't a man but a woman at the table. She was watching me, her lips pulled tight in a toothless smile. Amusement danced in her eyes, and a sense of fun showed up in the creases in the corners of her face. She was used to smiling.

"Hello," she said. Her lips pursed suggestively, her eyes dropped for a moment to my breasts then back to my mouth. She raised an eyebrow.

I asked her what she'd like to drink. She cocked her head on one side. Her eyes ran over my legs. She was appraising me. I was a feminised bimbo with my tits on show and, to all intents and purposes, no skirt. Maybe she preferred girls? Despite my over-the-top appearance, I suppose I looked good.

Her dark eyes glided over me one more time and she gave me her drink order. I missed it, I was transfixed by her. There was something about her I couldn't put my finger on. She drew me in. She was about my age, not traditionally pretty. Her nose was a little longer than average and her face thin and long. A few freckles ran across the bridge of her nose. She had long dark-red hair which she'd pulled back into a ponytail. A fringe hung straight to her eyebrows, parted in the middle. Her smooth knees protruded from cuts in each knee of her jeans. Her breasts were not large but pert under a white top with a loose neckline.

"S...s...sorry, Madam. Could you t..tell me

again," I stuttered.

She chuckled with a finger arched against her lips. My stomach rolled. I wouldn't have thought her my type. I was more my type, the way I looked now. But she had something. A lightness fluttered around inside my head.

"A diet coke and a chicken salad. And don't look so shocked, dear. I won't bite you...not yet anyway."

It took me a moment to register what she had said. Was she coming on to me? Me, looking like this? All boobs, bum, false vagina lips and not much else in the way of clothing. I decided she was amused at my appearance.

"Coming right up, Madam." I curtsied without thinking. Immediately I wished I could have rewound that moment. Elizabeth and

Fiona's training had kicked in automatically.

"Very formal. I like the curtsey, I could get used to that from a pretty..." She tilted her head again."Girl?"

What did that mean?

She held out a small slim hand, palm down. Her deep blue fingernails were neat, not too long. I shook her hand. It was cool and soft. There was something unusual about this woman; I was entranced. I had little chance with her looking like I did, trussed up like a cheap prostitute.

"And what's your name, pretty..." Her eyes flicked all over me. "Girl?"

There it was again. The questioning tone. She had spotted me as a male under this bimbo slut cover, I was sure. She seemed to be amused by the fact I was a feminised male. Amused, but not put off.

"It's Patricia, Madam." I went to curtsey again, but I stopped myself as I went to dip. I had been trained to speak to all women with respect, use a title and curtsey. It came naturally.

"A pretty name for a pretty girl. Pleased to meet you, Patricia." Her eyes dropped to my exposed panties then flicked up and widened for a moment. "And the curtsey?"

I dipped a small curtsey and meant it. She didn't introduce herself and I was unsure if I should ask her name. A few months ago, long months ago when I was male, I would have given her a cheeky grin and asked. I used to be confident of my strength of personality and charisma. I wanted to know who she was. She had something special that knotted my stomach. It wasn't just her friendliness. She was slim and not too tall but she filled the entire room.

"What's your name, Madam?"

Her eyebrows raised a touch. She was part focussed on her mobile phone, but I felt I also had her attention.

She stopped tapping on the screen for a moment and looked into my eyes. "I like that. Madam." She chewed it over. "Madam will do perfectly well, Patricia."

I rushed away, flushed. Was she coming on to me or teasing me? I went to the bar to get her drink, the background chatter lowered as eyes fell on me. Micaela slapped down the drink and glared. The pub was filling up. My breasts struggled to stay inside my top. I fidgeted with a finger inside my top to pull it over a nipple threatening again to break free. I'd have to speak to Elisabeth about finding a top that didn't risk imminent exposure. I placed a hand behind me, the tight hem of the pencil skirt dug in showing a half-moon of my bare bum.

I glanced back at the enigmatic lady. She was watching me with a faint smile. I collected her drink and typed her food order into the terminal. I pretended to concentrate on the task. From the corner of my eyes I saw her stare was trained on me like a heat-seeking missile.

I took orders from the other customers, enduring comments and stares, giggles and angry looks from the women. My six-inch heels clicked noisily on the polished wooden floor as I worked the room. It called attention to me. A couple of times a male hand brushed the exposed part of my bottom cheek. Deliberate? I wasn't sure, but I was sure I hated it and I hated Elizabeth. She had gone too far this time. I had to do something. I had no idea what, she controlled my clothing, money and accommodation.

The enigmatic lady ate alone. Once she had finished she got up and strode to the exit. I was clearing up another customer's dirty plates and glasses. I watched the lady move towards the door with a pang of disappointment. For the first time in a while, I wanted to be male again. She turned at the open door and gave a nod of her head, a tiny wave and she was gone. I was crestfallen, I'd hoped to speak to her again. She was gone.

I went to the round dark wooden table in the corner to clear her dishes away. I stacked them up. As I put her plate on top of a dish, I spotted a business card tucked under it. I leant forward to pick it up, aware it exposed more of my bottom attracting a room full of stares. I placed a hand there and pulled at the hem. I filled my lungs and breathed out deeply. I picked up the business card.

Elena Castle

Beneath her name was a mobile number, an email and various social media addresses. I turned the card over. There was a logo of a golden tower with battlements and a company name, Castle Designers, next to it. Below the name was a message written in green ink:

Pretty Patricia

You interest me.

We'll meet again

XXX

I hadn't expected that. My knees wobbled. What did she want with me? She had seen through my feminisation. I asked myself again: what did she want with me? My insides bubbled with excitement, I hadn't felt like this since Jackie with the luscious lips had promised my first blow job when I was sixteen.

I cleared away the plates and thought about this lady: Elena. It was almost 3 pm and I was due a break. I went out to the staff room behind the bar and sat at the rectangular Formica table. I was alone, my head swimming with Elena, or should I call her Madam Elena? I was thankful for some respite from the horror of serving customers while looking like an underdressed slut. I'd heard some use that word in stage whispers. The comments were about my breasts, my bum and the fake vagina lips. I had been the entertainment for the afternoon.

Elena Castle hadn't been like that. She seemed amused, but interested in me. Aloof, but kind. I didn't know why. My dreams were interrupted by Suzie entering the staff room. My head dropped. Her face was stern and I guessed what was coming.

"Stand up, Patty, and take down your knickers and unstrap yourself."

I had to masturbate again. She said I had to keep masculine sexual thoughts out of my mind and to clean myself of nasty male fluids. I complained, but Suzie told me Fiona wanted me cleaned out five times a day for the first day. She told me she had the unhappy task of overseeing two milkings at work and she had to do what her boss told her. I moved towards the storeroom. Suzie's hand pushed against my chest.

"No here is fine, Patty. You will milk yourself into a paper tissue and then clear up and get home to your wife."

She pursed her lips in thought.

"The customers love you, or to be more accurate, they love how you look."

Tension gripped my body. It was too open here. Any of the other staff could walk in on me masturbating. I opened my mouth to complain but a stiff slap caught my cheek leaving me gulping.

"Get on with it, Patty. You don't think I enjoy seeing you beating your little thing, do you?"

I glanced at the open doorway to the bar, willing and hoping no one came through. I pulled my panties down and the fake vagina lips came with them. I pulled away the tape holding my penis tight against my crotch. It fell away with a deep sense of relief and life flowed back into it. Suzie sniggered at my flaccid penis, fully exposed beneath the hem of my tiny pencil skirt.

She giggled again at my lack of balls, still pushed up inside my body. I took my penis and began to rub against the foreskin. I didn't feel like cumming. This would be the third time today; I had a problem getting erect.

A slap across my penis shook me out of my stupor. "Rub harder, stupid girl. You're not leaving here until you cum."

For some reason, I found this something of a turn on and I began to get erect.

"Better," she said.

This too had an effect and I jerked to full attention.

"I see you like a woman telling you what to do." Suzie was satisfied.

The tingling on my nether regions told me I was building up to ejaculate. Suzie watched intently.

"There's a good girl," she murmured. She sounded kinder and for an instant, it seemed she was helping me.

I came into the tissue.

"Wipe up the dregs, girly."

Her voice dragged back me to reality. My moment of pleasure fell away. I was standing with my cum pooled in a tissue, a limp penis and panties around my knees. Things couldn't get any worse, could they?

Chapter 7 - Feminized and slutty

I got home late afternoon and Elizabeth allowed me to go to my room to relax. My first day at work in my new slutty clothing style had been traumatic. I was pleased with the space to come to terms with it. I may as well have gone to work naked such was the tiny size of my new clothing. I'd endured comments, touching and stares. My minute skirt and top left little to the imagination. Men thought this gave them licence to touch and talk about me.

My room become more claustrophobic than ever. It was difficult to understand why a house so large as Elizabeth's had such a tiny room. My single bed hugged one plain pink painted wall giving me about two feet of space on the other side. A shaft of light from the hall landing glared into my room through the door-less entrance. Elizabeth permitted no secrecy, no privacy. A plain single wardrobe sat against the other side, the open front revealing my humiliation. Short dresses and tiny skirts hung from the bar on white plastic hangers. The whole house dripped in luxury, except my prison cell-like bedroom.

Elisabeth came into my room without warning, I hadn't heard her in the hallway outside. She granted me one hour to relax, but this was impossible. It was a relief to get off my feet and lay on the bed. And I was still padlocked into my six-inch heels, never permitted to walk in anything else. I even had to sleep in them.

I sat up. I pleaded with my wife to allow to change into a longer skirt for work. A skirt that actually covered my panties. I wanted to look pretty but this new style was slutty in the extreme.

Elizabeth told me to beg for different clothing. She enjoyed hearing me tell her I wanted to wear a pretty skirt. The truth was, I did want to wear a skirt but I wanted one that flowed around my thighs. I didn't want a skirt that covered nothing but the bottom of my stomach. I longed for the swirl of soft cotton lapping around my legs as I walked.

She agreed. That was a shock. A surge of love fell over me. My eagerness made me expose my desire for feminisation again: a fatal mistake. I couldn't believe she had granted permission to wear something more comfortable than a 4-inch pencil skirt. Why should I should feel love for

Elizabeth? She treated me poorly. This was something I couldn't understand. Maybe it was some form of Stockholm Syndrome?

She said she was going to permit me to wear something longer. I hoped it was something that gave me relief from the utter humiliation of my panties and bum being displayed. My desperation to wear a pretty skirt was an example of how far she had taken me along the path to femininity. My relief was temporary. I should have known Elizabeth had something else in store for me. She knew I now embraced my feminisation and she didn't want me to enjoy anything.

She passed me a pretty flowery skirt. This was a positive step. It was longer and feminine.

"Remove your little pencil skirt and panties,"

she said.

I did this with relish. I ripped them off and pulled on the flowery skirt. The front was cut away and the skirt fell either side of my penis and balls. My penis was framed leaving me fully exposed.

"Your clitty and pussy balls will remain exposed at home at all times." She looked at my genitals with a sweet expression. "Your clitty is a *cute little princess.*"

She observed my penis a while longer. I withered at the stare.

"I've had some of your dresses and skirts adapted to have an open front. They will show your *little princess* in all its cuteness."

I groaned in helplessness. I tried to breathe out but the corset restricted my ribs. This had to remain on too. It gave me a defined hourglass figure.

Elizabeth leant to me and pulled the front of my top down.

"You are to leave your pretty breasts exposed at home too. I paid a lot of money for them, I want to see the benefit of my investment."

She turned and left without another word. I lay back on my bed, my huge firm breasts protruded up from my chest and my penis and balls fell against my legs. Everything was on show. I despaired. This was worse than before.

I glanced at my bedside clock: nearly 7 pm. At any minute, Clara would be coming to oversee my fourth milking of the day. I didn't think I could manage any more ejaculations. I was spent. My feminisation at the hands of Elizabeth was turning into something much darker. I understand why she wanted to punish me but she had done that. I didn't understand why she was taking it so much further.

I turned Elena's business card over in my hand like a card sharp at a casino. I wanted to call her to find out what she wanted from me. To find out what she had found so interesting, apart from the obvious amusement angle. It didn't seem she was like Elizabeth though, there appeared to be an interest in me.

A shadow blocked the hall light and Clara walked into the room. She motioned for me to stand. I jumped off the bed to avoid any risk of punishment and lost my balance on my heels. Regaining some stability, I curtsied. Clara had blue rubber kitchen gloves on, I knew what was coming.

Clara milked me mechanically into a plastic container. It was as if she was milking a cow as I bent over above the container. She held the base of my penis with one hand and tugged back and forth on my erection with the other. It took me some effort but eventually thin slivers of thin cum dripped against the bottom of the plastic. My head went down as my penis hung limply and defeated between the open sides of my altered skirt. My 42-inch DD boobs stuck out impossibly pert for a chest so large.

Clara passed me a wet wipe and told me to clean myself up. I kept my head bowed. My throat was tight as I cleaned my exhausted penis. I dropped the wet wipe in the container. Clara remained standing, her hands on her hips. She wanted something more.

"Drink up your cum, girl, and lick out the container. Nice and clean." Her eyes pierced into me.

That was an unpleasant scenario. I had no choice. I raised the container to my lips with distaste and instantly pulled it away again. A smell of damp chlorine mixed with plastic flowed into my nostrils. I dry heaved.

"Hurry up, Elizabeth wants you downstairs looking pretty. She doesn't want you with any nasty erections or drips. Erections aren't feminine, are they."

My head spun up. Why would she want me downstairs? And ready for what exactly? She slapped my face which didn't answer my questions but reminded me of the distasteful thing Clara wanted me to do: to drink my cum.

I tipped the container up and a cold thick liquid touched my lips. It reminded me of mucus. The smell of dampness and salt seemed to hang in the air. At least there wasn't much after three previous ejaculations today. I wouldn't have thought it possible at the age of thirty-six to cum four times in one day.

I tipped the container into my mouth. The gooey cold substance dripped onto my tongue and I shivered. I swallowed and my entire body shook once. A sweet taste hung in the back of my throat.

"Lick the bowl clean, Patty."

I ran my tongue around the container. I tasted metal and cum. I swallowed again and shuddered. Clara's eyebrows raised in a sign of approval. She surprised me by kneeling in front of me, her eyes level with my penis. A blow job was out of the question, even if she tried.

She held a cigar-sized metal tube. It was open both ends like a pipe with a small hinge on one side and a tiny catch with a miniature padlock on the other. The tube was around four inches long. She waved it at me. I had no idea what it was for.

She pulled my foreskin back and held it there tight. My delicate cone-shaped penis head was red and shrivelled. She put the metal tube around the stem of my penis trapping the retracted foreskin under the tube. She clipped the little padlock shut, my foreskin held tight under the tube. She sat back to admire her work.

My penis was encased inside the metal tube

from the end of the head to the base by the top of my balls. It had the effect of making my penis poke out at right angles from my triangular pubic mound. Cool air licked around my sensitive gland. I felt even more exposed.

Clara leant back in to look, pleased with her work. She tied a small pink ribbon around the base of my balls and finished it in a bow on the top of my metal-encased penis. The loops of the bow made two perfect hoops.

She unclipped the top of a blue marker pen and drew two small eyes on the top of my exposed penis head. I flinched at the scratch of the felt-tipped marker against my sensitive tender skin. My eyes watered and then widened at each new debasement of me. Clara leant back again and nodded with approval at her work.

She put the blue pen down and picked up a red marker pen. She drew a line below the 'eyes' along my penis slit once, then again. I wasn't able to see what she'd done. She stifled a giggle.

She scratched the pen under my slit twice in what felt like two bow shapes. Clara's tongue protruded from the corner of her mouth in concentration. I wanted to pull away from the excruciating feeling of the pen dragging against my gland. She giggled, not attempting to hide it. She lifted a small make-up mirror for me to see.

She had drawn a small face with a smile on my penis head. Was there no end to my degradation and humiliation? At least the word *clitty* was hidden by the metal tube. My concern now was it stood out straight like a pointing finger. My exposed head led the way, the smiling face she'd drawn adding to my utter humiliation.

Clara stood, her eyes fixed on my encased penis with its cartoon face. She lifted it with a finger, a smirk on the corner of her mouth. She dropped my penis and ran two fingers of each hand over my enormous breasts and across my nipples. A tingle of electricity shot to my stomach. This was a new feeling; my nipples had become more sensitive. It was nice.

"OK, you're ready to be presented, Patty."

"Presented, what do you mean presented? To who?"

Clara slapped my face once. I'd forgotten to call her Mistress in my distress. I apologised meekly.

"To *whom,* Patty, remember your grammar." She laughed at her own joke. "So, Patty, let's go downstairs and find the answer to your question, shall we?"

She led me downstairs, my open skirt flicking against my thighs, my encased penis swaying from side to side. My exposed breasts bounced lightly with each step.

Chapter 8 – Girl's night

As we descended the stairs, the murmur of female voices increased in volume. My exposed penis and breasts bounced up and down as I negotiated each step. Although I now walked well in my six-inch heels, I still found going down the stairs difficult. I went down sideways, gripping the bannister to avoid slipping.

My platinum blond hair tousled around my breasts. It framed them like a bizarre-looking mermaid from the waist up. We reached the downstairs hall and I could hear the soft chatter of female voices from the front room. I hadn't heard anyone arrive. The living room door was closed but I guessed there were between six to eight different voices. They seemed to be all talking at once.

The light was fading outside as clouds darkened and dusk fell. Pats of rain splatted against the glazed front door. The wind whistled outside like an angry wasp trapped in a bottle. A late summer August storm was brewing. I shivered. A mix of the weather and the coming humiliation that waited behind the door.

Clara knocked on the living-room door and the buzz of voices reduced in level. It was as if someone had turned down a volume switch. Her hand went to the handle but she didn't open it immediately.

"Ladies, ladies." It was Elizabeth's voice on the other side of the door followed by the ring of metal against glass. A couple of sounds of shushes hissed. Silence followed. "As you all know, I'm a demanding lady." A couple of sniggers sounded and Clara grinned at me. "You also know my opinion of men." This time laughter rang out. "Men should be seen and not heard. The more subservient the better." A ripple of applause greeted her words.

Clara looked around at me, her hand still grasping the handle, listening at the door but waiting.

"What you may not know, apart from Fiona of course, is I believe men are so much better when feminised." A few questioning sounds came up. "By feminised, I mean put in pretty female clothes — skirts dresses and so on. We should make them grow their hair and have it styled in feminine ways. We should put them into high heels, stockings. Yes, they should look like pretty girls."

A murmur rose. Some voices squealed with delight and there was a light clapping.

Elizabeth continued. "Feminisation not only makes men more attractive, but also makes them better behaved and more submissive. We all want that in a man don't we?"

A couple of cries of '*yes we*' do rang out.

"So, let me introduce my husband. He, or should that be she? I'll call her, she. She will serve us tonight, submissive, exposed and feminised and pretty. And completely under my control. Clara, if you please."

Clara twisted the door handle. What on earth was going on? What was this all about? I was going to find out in a few moments as Clara swung open the door. I stepped back and slunk behind the door, out of sight. What was this? Was I now an exhibit for my wife to show off?

Elizabeth came towards me, her heels clipping on the floor. She stopped in the doorway. I gazed at her, not an ounce of fat on her slim body, well-built and strong. Her legs were slim and toned. I cowered and peeked around the door. I expected anger, but she had a gentle expression on her face, the look of a mother for a child.

"Come on, Patricia, don't be shy. I want to show you to my friends, there's a good girl."

She reached out a hand. She'd never held my hand before. An excited chatter of female voices rose from the living room.

My instant reaction was to drape one arm across my enormous breasts and the other over my exposed penis. I didn't want to go into the room looking like this. I was a man with 42DD tits, a female hairstyle and an exposed penis head. The metal tube was uncomfortable around my penis. My trapped foreskin was sore and I didn't like my sensitive penis head exposed. The slightest knock would be uncomfortable, even painful.

The tube prevented me from getting hard. It was a cock cage with maximum humiliation. The cartoon face Clara had drawn on it made the situation worse.

Elizabeth pulled at my hand and dragged me into the room; I staggered in my heels. My ankle gave way making it a less than elegant entrance. My arrival was met by instant wild female screams. I looked up slowly. There were ten women scattered around the living room. Some stood, some sat. My eyes met Fiona's, satisfaction was etched across her face. I didn't know the other women.

I tried to step back. My mouth went dry and I swallowed in a vain attempt to generate some saliva. Elizabeth held onto my hand with a firm grip. She led me to the centre of the room where, except for Fiona, they gathered around me in an arc.

Their eyes fell all over me, drinking in the spectacle of my exaggerated female body with my penis exhibited in a metal tube. Elizabeth lifted my encased penis to display it better to the eager eyes.

"When you feminise your husband, you need to deal with the *little princess,*" Elizabeth announced.

I closed my eyes, this had to be a bad dream.

"Look at the little face on the end of his willy." One of the ladies screamed out causing more laughter. The room was in uproar. Pandemonium. I scrunched my eyes tighter, I wanted to shut out the world and fall through the floor into another world.

"Ladies." It was Elizabeth calling above the noise. She was still holding my penis tube for the audience. "This is how a husband should look. Please feel free to poke and touch but remember, my husband is now a female so refer to her as such. She doesn't have a willy or a penis. It's a *clitty* or a *cute princess*."

I kept my eyes closed. I wanted to hide. Fingers passed over my tits and nipples. I felt my balls being poked and probed. A finger stroked the end of my penis then squeezed it hard. I jumped in surprise which caused more laughter.

After a few minutes, the frenzy calmed and the ladies took their seats. I had no idea who they were and Elizabeth didn't seem in any hurry to explain why she was displaying me to them.

"Ladies, since Patty is now a trained waitress, she will serve us for the evening. She will take your drinks orders."

I didn't know who this group were, I guessed by their look they were in business. Every time I think she'd gone to the extreme, she went further and pushed the boundaries way beyond what was acceptable. Elizabeth had no limits. I had to be worried about how much further she would go with my humiliation. The ladies passed a list round and one of them handed it to me. I scuttled out to the kitchen to get their drinks orders.

Outside the summer storm reached a peak and thunder crashed above us. The windows rattled. This was worse than Fiona's pub. Or better?

Chapter 9 - A mistress and a meeting

Warm humid dampness filled the gastropub the next day. The daily grind of travelling and working in tiny skirts was excruciating. My breasts fell out of my top constantly and were a magnet for leering lustful eyes. After last night's humiliation with Elizabeth's friends, at least I had some cover.

That morning, an early morning freshness announced the beginning of September. This had consequences for my nipples. They poked out firmly through the thin material.

A gloomy midday light forced its way through the small squares of the misted Georgian windows at the front of the pub. Outside, a storm raged. The past week had alternated between heavy rain and sun. Wet umbrellas and jackets dripped onto the floor from a stand by the dark wooden front doors.

I slapped down three plates filled with large burgers and fried potatoes onto a round table. The men jumped in their seats. My mind was elsewhere and I was only vaguely aware of their stares washing over my breasts. A nipple had burst out but I gave up the fight.

I'd had a brainwave after I found a small white apron in the pub storeroom. I'd tied it around my waist. Although short, it covered the front of my panties and false vagina lips. I let the ties fall long down the back and this provided some cover over my exposed bum. I'd expected Suzie to tell me to take it off, but she had smiled on seeing it and said nothing.

I wore a tiny pink tartan skirt with small sharp pencil pleats. It was tight around my high waits and no more than three inches long so I was pleased to have found the apron. I had a tight white cotton top on and it clung to my breasts like heat-shrunk film. The low front cut across my nipples and exposed enough of each of my dark areolae to lusting stares. I poked the nipple back into until next time.

I was out of ideas, out of plans, out of hope. Clara had masturbated me mechanically for my three-a-day milking regime at home and Suzie at work. The humiliation was giving way to an accepted unloved routine. It was like going to work at a job you hate. You do it as there's no alternative.

A single tear dripped down my cheek. Was it

the damp heat or deep sadness? A finger brushed against my cheek and wiped away my tear. For a short moment, I didn't register what had happened. My focus was in a distant nothingness.

I looked up. Elena.

She observed me for a moment "I've only popped in to see you, Patty. I'm not stopping. What time do you finish today, pretty girl?"

I swallowed hard. "5.30? Why?"

"Great. I'll be waiting for you outside. 5.30 on the bench opposite, across the road."

I hesitated thinking about what Elizabeth's reaction would be if I was late home. Elena saw I was thinking of something.

"What's up, pretty Patricia?"

I explained my wife was a demanding person

and I would have problems if I was late home. Instantly I was angry with myself for letting out I had a wife. I thought I should get to know Elena better before admitting my true self to her.

One of Elena's eyebrows raised. "Don't worry, pretty Patricia, give me her phone number and I'll let her know you'll be late."

She pulled her phone from her handbag and tapped at the screen for a few moments. She passed it to me, open on the contact page. "Type her name and mobile number in here and I'll give her a call and make sure you won't get into trouble."

I took the phone but my finger froze over the keyboard. "Elena, you don't know what she's like. I don't want to get into trouble." I stared into her eyes imploring her to be careful.

"Don't worry, Patricia, it'll be fine. Don't worry. Type your wife's phone number in my phone and then be a good girl and run along."

Elena took her phone back after I'd tapped in Elizabeth's number. Elena glanced at the number for an instant, waved, and left the pub. The door closed behind her slowly. I waited a few moments wishing she had stayed.

A shaft of sunlight peered in through the windows. The storm had passed over. Distant thunder rumbled, each roar sounded further away.

The afternoon passed slowly as I counted down the minutes to my meeting with Elena. I didn't want to be too excited. Elena's manner and actions hadn't shown anything other than being amused by me. I wanted there to be something else and this carried me on. Something told me I intrigued her. She'd seen through my over-the-top feminisation instantly. If she had any doubts, my reference to Elizabeth as my wife confirmed I was still biologically a male under all this feminisation. But what did she want from me?

5.30 arrived and I untied my little white apron and threw it across the bar. I went into the staff toilets. I looked into the cracked mirror above a stained metal sink. The tap dripped. I took a small hairbrush from my white leather handbag. Elizabeth may be treating me badly but she is happy to provide feminine items for me to use.

I restyled my platinum-blond hair and fluffed it up with my fingers. It glistened under the small fluorescent lamp above the mirror. I brushed at my hair, the waves sprung back after five and a half hours working in the humid room of the pub. I stood to one side to brush my hair down to the small of my back. I positioned my hair over my cleavage with my fingers, to give some coverage. There was nothing I could do about the vagina shape showing through my panties below the useless skirt.

My permanent smokey eye make-up was perfect, as it should be. I flicked my super-long black false eyelashes in the hard light. They make my eyes look sleepy and sultry. My sharp chiselled cheeks and strong jaw broke what should have been a perfect feminine image. My wide shoulders drooped as I told myself to be positive. I was sure Elena was a positive force. I straightened up and pushed my shoulders back up. I sprayed a little perfume on my neck and I strode out of the toilets.

I clipped out of the front door of the pub, a sea of male eyes followed every step of my heels. The tiny padlocks flapped against my ankles. The bright evening sunlight was lower in the sky and I made a peak over my eyes with one hand. The summer storm had long gone and a warm evening sun had burned away the dampness. I scanned the other side of the road looking for the bench where Elena had said she would be waiting. It was empty and my shoulders dropped again.

What had I expected? She was probably playing with me, teasing me. Who would want a person like me? I was a submissive feminised

Barbie Doll with giant tits and a frill for a skirt. I pondered my options. There would be no harm in waiting for a while.

I smoothed down my pink pleated skirt for no reasons, it was not about to get any longer. I marched across the road and sat on the bench. I crossed my smooth bare legs and placed my handbag over my fake vagina shape. Sitting down, the skirt covered me a little better.

I looked to the sky. White wisps of cloud spread high in the sky like splashes of split milk on a blue ceramic tile. I closed my eyes to shut out the world. The lightest of breezes fluffed my hair. It brushed against my taut cleavage skin and across my sensitive areolae. It was a gentle pleasant tickling sensation. Erotic. I imagined Elena's finger lightly tracing my erect nipples.

My flattened taped-up penis tried to expand inside the tube but failed.

I wondered if Elena would come. If she did come, what exactly would she want from me?

Chapter 10 – Girls like him

A voice broke into my daydreams. "Patricia."

I looked around. A woman's figure was shadowed in front of the low sun. An aura of light surrounded her head and made her hair appear bright red. She sat beside me.

"You looked like you were enjoying yourself sitting there thinking, Patricia."

My stomach somersaulted; I nodded bashfully. She took my hand in both of hers. Her hands were slim and small over my large palm. Her nails were shorter than mine and shone from the blue lacquer. They clashed with my long talons coloured in bright luminous pink.

She was wore a light blue dress to her knees. Her grey shoes had short heels. Her red hair hung to her shoulders. There was no hint of a curl, suggesting she straightened it. She wore simple silver studs in each earlobe with three small rings above them. Apart from some eyelash colour and a little foundation, she had no make-up on her chalk-white face. She had no wrinkles until she smiled.

"Let's go for a coffee and a chat. I want to find out more about you, Patricia."

She let go of my hands and stood. I remained seated, frozen to the spot. I inspected my tingling hands, still sensitive from her touch. This was the first kindness anyone had shown for several months; I found it difficult to take it in. But what did she want? I liked her interest but I had to be careful not to let this drag me into any false hope.

I stood and she turned and walked towards the centre of town expecting me to follow. I shook my head and trotted in her wake. She didn't take my hand and I walked by her side, like two girls out for a stroll. I got looks and attention although the stares were for my huge bursting breasts and vagina-shaped panties.

We turned down a single lane off the high street and into an independent coffee shop. Once inside, she stopped and pulled a ten-pound note from her handbag.

"Get me an Americano and whatever you want. Bring it to me over there." She pointed to an empty round table with two chairs in the corner.

I fought against curtseying, her eyes danced with amusement. I went to the counter and gave the order to the young man behind the counter. He never took his eyes from my cleavage. I paid, picked up the coffees, and went over to her. I sat opposite.

"No," she said. "Pull your chair around and sit next to me."

I did as she asked.

She watched me for a moment. "I called your wife and she said it was no problem for us to meet. She said she's happy for you to have female friends to discuss female things with, like clothing and make-up. I told her I wanted to take you shopping for girly things and to have beauty work done, such as nails and hair. She was pleased. Would you like that, pretty girl?"

My face reddened instantly, my neck and cheeks felt hot. The opportunity to have a small break from Elizabeth's humiliations sounded wonderful. Doing girly things with Elena sounded boring but better than spending time with Elizabeth. I mumbled a thank you. I still didn't understand what Elena wanted from me but her gentle assertiveness was magnetic.

Although her card had described her as a company owner, like Elizabeth, she did not have the hard businesswoman style of my wife. She had something more creative, more welcoming. There was something else – an amused look that sparkled in her eyes.

She looked down at my legs and slid the back of her hand up my thigh. Her fingers reached my exposed panties. She tapped her nail once on my fake vagina lips and withdrew her hand.

"I like girls like you, Patty."

I had hardly said a word since we'd met. I had to say something, to ask her what she wanted from me. "Elena, what is it I can do for you?"

Her eyebrows raised. "Patricia, dear."

She took my hand again with two of hers. The softness of her hands on mine, the gentle touch threw a desperate urge flying into my taped-up penis. It had nowhere to go. The tape and my tubular cock cage kept me restrained. I was pleased to have some kind of urge after the milkings today. Somewhere deep inside, my masculinity stirred. Despite my almost complete feminisation and emasculation, I was attracted to this beautiful woman.

She'd asked me something but I missed it as I mused on my attraction to her and her kindness. "I'm sorry, I was miles away. I was enjoying being here with you. It's been a long time since a pretty woman held my hand."

Elena sat back and kept hold of my hand. She looked out the window. "I have a hunch your wife feminised you because of your poor behaviour?" Her head turned back towards me.

Heat rose in my neck. There was something new in her voice, a toughness I hadn't heard before from her.

"Well, Patricia, am I right?" Her voice was soft with a hint of command behind it.

I hadn't expected her to be so direct even though she'd seen through my feminine facade. "Er yes." It was the only reply I could manage. She was kindly but firm.

Her hands tightened on mine."I thought so.

You still have some rough edges to polish off." She regarded me with an evaluating look. Her mind was turning over as if recalculating her thoughts. "With a bit of caring effort, I could get you there. You need someone to coach and care for you, not punish you."

I was put off for a moment. "Excuse me, Elena?"

"You're to call me Madam. Never Elena."

I stuttered a couple of times. "Yes, Madam. Of course."

This was no hardship although I was disappointed to have to call her Madam. Or was I? What was it she saw in me? What was it about me that said I needed a woman to feminise me? It was clear her conversation with Elizabeth was wider than about going for a drink to discuss make-up.

A few minutes passed in silence. Elena looked outside and things became uncomfortable. I hoped I hadn't annoyed her before a friendship could develop. But, she was another lady who liked feminised men. The difference was she was far gentler than Elizabeth. Even before my feminisation, Elizabeth was never warm and loving. Elena was kind but had a touch of steel covered in cotton wool.

"Why does Elizabeth insist you wear such revealing clothing, Patricia?" She turned back to me. "And why the giant boobs? Has she removed your penis? Are you on hormones?"

Her questions fired at me like a machine gun. I explained the back story to my feminisation. I told her my penis was fully functional and I didn't take female hormones. I didn't tell her about the milking humiliation. She responded with more silence and gazed again out the window. The roar of the coffee maker behind the counter filled the room. I was learning this was her style; she liked to take time to think.

"If you were mine, I'd still want you to wear pretty skirts, that much would not change. You would look more feminine if they were a little longer. Mid-thigh would be about right. You'd look cute in a pretty summer dress. Short, but not like you wear now. I prefer heels a little lower, four inches? What do you say, Patricia? Would you like to wear pretty mini skirts and dresses for me?"

"Yes, I would, Madam." My garbled reply

came out too quickly, too enthusiastically. Her face beamed. I'd given away too much. Next to us, two young girls listened in rapt fascination. I tried to ignore them.

"Great," she replied then looked at her watch. "I have to go now, Princess. It's been lovely to chat but I have a business to run." She got up to leave.

I stood sharply. I was confused.

"Madam Elena, what next? I don't understand. What do you want from me?" The two girls followed our every move and word.

"I don't need anything from anyone, Princess, but I have a feeling you may be what I've been looking for. Next time we'll do some girly shopping together. What do you say?"

I nodded enthusiastically. I wanted to be

with her, to find any excuse to spend time together, even shopping. Elena kissed me on my cheek, brushing my lips. Desire burned through me. I was hooked.

"We'll be meeting often, pretty princess. Shame you already have a mistress but let's see."

She left. I remained standing. My appearance attracted the usual looks and giggles. I left the coffee shop a few seconds after Elena. She was already out of sight. I strode to the station on my way home. For the first time in several weeks there was a spring in my step and a low yellow sun warmed my face

Chapter 11 - Sissy sensations

Elena and I started to meet regularly after I finished work. Elizabeth liked my relationship with Elena. She didn't know I had fallen for my new friend. She didn't consider this and saw it as me having a female friend and doing girly things together. This was how Elena had sold to her.

Elizabeth approved of the finger and toenail work Elena had persuaded me to have. I had swirling patterns in shades of pink and sparkling jewellery in each of my long fingernails. It was extremely feminine but I was happy.

Elena began to call for me at home some weekends with Elizabeth's agreement. The first time she'd arrived at the front door, she had been shocked at what I was wearing. I wore a small frilly skirt, open at the front and displaying the tubular cock cage. She spotted the cartoon face Clara delighted in drawing on the end of my tender exposed penis gland. Sometimes Clara drew large ears in black ink on either side of my penis to make it look like an elephant's trunk. My huge boobs were exposed, supported by the under bra.

Elena got on well with Elizabeth, which surprised me. She never stayed long, always taking me out somewhere. Elizabeth respected Elena as she was also a company owner. They often discussed how to make me more feminine. Elizabeth loved Elena's idea about how I should date men. Elena promised she would try to find someone for me. A nice handsome man, she said.

Elena's reasons for this story were soon

apparent. She asked Elizabeth to remove my metal cage whenever we go out. "In case Patricia gets lucky and we find nice young man who wants to suck it.," she told my wife.

Elena soothed my horror at this idea when we were at the hairdresser's salon. I was having my roots done and new waves put in. As I sat with curlers in, Elena explained she had no intention of finding me a man. It was a story for Elizabeth. She had other ideas for me. I asked what they were. She smiled and told me to wait and see. She tapped the end of my nose playfully.

One Saturday, a few days later, Elena arranged to come to the house to take me out. After a short chat with Elizabeth, she said she was taking me for dinner at a restaurant by the river in the evening. She told Elizabeth it was always full of young men and they often hit on her. She explained it might be a great way to introduce me to someone. She told Elizabeth I might not be home if I got lucky. Elizabeth was ecstatic and trusted Elena. Although Elena had told me she wouldn't introduce me to men, I didn't like the sound of this. I was happy she removed my cage though.

Elizabeth suggested a pretty yellow patterned summer dress. It had thin straps hooked over my shoulders and held up a low-fronted dress top. Two mall triangular pieces of the dress just about covered my nipples and I had no bra on. She picked flesh coloured hold up stockings, the tops showed as I walked.

We didn't go to the restaurant by the river. Elena drove me to her home. It was twenty miles outside the city in a small commuter town. Her home was a red-brick renovated Edwardian townhouse. She'd restored the original features had been restored and had wide oak floorboards, ornate white coving and black metal fireplaces in every room except the ultra-modern kitchen.

Elena told me to sit on the living room sofa. It was wide and soft. I sank into it. She put a vinyl disc on the record deck. Light classical music filled the room. She sat next to me, our legs and arms touched and my heart jumped. Elena wore high-waisted light trousers and I couldn't feel her flesh. I ached for it anyway.

She moved a hand onto my leg and stroked it. She moved her fingers to the top of my stockings. She placed her other arm over my shoulder. Clara had milked me twice earlier in the day but Elena's scent and proximity caused a hardening in my tired penis.

I moved to kiss her, I was desperate to draw her in, to taste her. I wanted to feel her lips, her breath and her tongue. She pulled back. A momentary flash of anger fell over her face. It melted into a calmness. "Wait, pretty girl. I lead, not you. I'll tell you when I want you to do something." She was gentle but firm.

She slid her hand under my dress. I willed it up to my waiting hard penis. It had been many months since it had been caressed lovingly by caring female hands. My erection pushed up in my tiny panties and tented the yellow dress. Elena spotted this and giggled. Goosebumps ran along my thigh and the back of my neck. I wanted her fingers on my penis — to stroke it. To give me affection.

She removed her hand. A pang of disappointment shot through me. She brushed her fingers over my tented erection and a spark shot straight to my stomach like an electric bolt. She moved her hand on and a pang of disappointment fell on me. I yearned for her touch. She was teasing me.

Her eyes hovered on my face, her other hand on the back of my neck under my thick blond hair. She removed her hand, pulled at her ponytail and flicked her head. Her red hair flowed out around her chalk-white face like flames on an open fire.

She stroked my neck and her other hand flicked over my stomach. Her touch was so light I could barely feel it, even through the thin cotton of my dress. She moved her hand to the bottom of my right bosom. My 42DD breasts strained. Two triangles of material pulled over my breasts, stretching the seams. My nipples were erect and firm through the material, so fine and tight it seemed like a second skin.

Her hand flowed up and cupped around the front of breast. She pressed a palm over it. She closed her fingers around my nipple and tweaked. A surge of electric sparks swirled my breast and down to my erection.

I let my mouth fall open and my throat closed. Where had this ecstasy come from? I'd never known those sensations on my nipples before. Was I now a real girl? My feelings were changing. This was all new.

She slipped her fingers inside my dress

front,and the skin of her fingertips rubbed on my taut breast skin. I jolted from the unexpected joy. She arched her hand and pushed down on my mound of fat and silicone implant. She twisted her hand and the dress material slid off to the side of my breast to expose an enormous mountain of taut flesh. She slid my shoulder straps off and the other part of the dress front fell away. Both my breasts were free. She ran her eyes over them, a strange look of success on her face.

She dipped her head to one of my erect nipples. Her lips pursed around it and I felt her tongue lick it. She sucked and put her teeth around it. The ecstasy flooded through me again. If this is what it meant to be a girl, I didn't want to return to masculinity.

I felt her other hand move down my body while she sucked and bit on my nipple. I groaned and closed my eyes, feeling them go up into my head. Her hand rested over my tented erection. I gasped again. She squeezed the end through the dress, reminding me I was a male. I had the best of both worlds.

Elena sucked and licked my nipple, then moved to the other. The sensation was intense. My straining erection, trapped under my little dress. Elena squeezed my erection as her tongue swirled around my nipple. I was going to explode if she kept that up.

She reached under my dress and hoisted it up to my stomach. She got up and tugged my panties down. She tossed them aside and looked down at my throbbing erection. "Oh my, you are excited, Patty."

My desperation for her was sky high. I wanted her mouth on my hard penis-clitty. She stood up, her eyes lit with amusement.

"Wait there, Patty. Don't go away."

There was no fear of that. She sped off to another room. I heard her climb the stairs and return a few minutes later. She re-entered the room. She had a black leather belt around her stomach. Protruding from it was a large life-like rubber penis.

"Bend over, turn around and lift your dress. It's time to experience penetration like a good girl."

This was not what I'd expected. Penetration? That sounded painful, especially with a huge rubber dildo. "I'm not sure, Elena, I mean,

Madam. It looks a large." My eyes settled on her strap-on cock. It looked to be at least eight inches long. Its girth looked all wrong on Elena's slim boyish frame. My eyes watered at the sight and the thought of what she was planning to do with it. Where she wanted to put it.

"You'll get used to it. In fact, you need to get used to it and eventually to enjoy it. Now, Patty, I won't ask again." Her voice was calm, tender but authoritative.

I wanted her to play with my breasts, fondle my erection, not insert a monstrously large cock into my bottom.

"I'll be gentle, I can assure you you're going to like this in time."

She hadn't shown any aggressive tendencies up to now. The opposite. I bent over and she came up behind me. The cool touch of the fake cock and something gel-like touched my anus ring. My erection jerked. Was I interested after all?

She told me to relax as I seemed tense. I was.

I bent over as she asked. It was humiliating to expose my naked bum to here but it was Elena. Far better than Clara. Or my horrible wife.

Without warning, she pushed the dildo an inch inside me. After the initial shock and a jab of pain, I found I had sensors and nerves I didn't know about. The pleasure raced to my stomach and penis. As she entered me, my muscles stretched beyond what they had ever experienced before. There was some discomfort, despite the cool lubrication she had applied. The incredible sensation and her gentleness and care outweighed any pain as she pushed deeper inside.

It was as if I were filling up. She took her time, allowing each inch of my hole to become used to the strap-on cock invading me. A friendly invasion. She pushed on and on, deeper and deeper, inch by inch. Zings of intense pleasure enveloped me as she hit against something deep inside me. She slid back out a little then pushed in again. To the hilt.

Again and again, she moved in and out. Slowly, carefully with more energy. Feelings and emotions I'd never felt before flowed through and over me. Each thrust sent waves of pleasure coursing around my body. I built to a point of no return and exploded onto the floor.

Elena withdrew and sat by me as I got my

breath back. Her huge dildo pointing to the ceiling "You enjoyed it. Good. This going to work for us. Now, clear your mess up and then make us a nice tea, there's a good girl."

I took a few moments to recover. What had just happened to me?

Chapter 12 - Sissy love

The next weekend Elena took me to her home again. When we entered she produced a pink maid's dress. She told me to put it on. I put it on without debate. She then told me to clean her kitchen and do her housework for her before we could play again. It was a small price to pay. Once I'd finished, we made love on her bed this time. Or should I say, she entered me again with her strap-on. The second time was easier. I knew what to expect and was more relaxed. I came hard into a towel she'd placed below me before she pumped me

As I recovered, Elena removed her jeans and panties. I stared in shock, this was what I wanted. She kept her top on but sat on the side of the bed. As I stared in surprise as she opened her legs wide. Her vagina lips parted invitingly. I was deflated. I'd cum again when she pegged me, this had been the second time I'd ejaculated that day. Clara had milked me in the morning. I apologised, I couldn't get an erection, I needed time to recover.

Elena laughed. "You're not going to put your *little clitty* in me, Princess. You're not a real man any more so that's never going to happen. When I want that, I'll find a real man. No, you're going to give me pleasure with your tongue. This will be your duty."

My entire stiffened at the thought of her having sex with a real man. I had little time to think when Elena laid back and pointed to her open sex. I moved in eagerly and the image of an alpha man with my Elena faded. I smelled soap and woman. She was already moist when my tongue flicked out to touch her swollen clitoris.

She moaned softly, "Good girl."

I sucked her clitoris into my mouth and she mumbled, "Good, good." She ordered me to roll my tongue around her erect clitoris and it grew further in my mouth. I then let it go and licked around the inside of her labia. She pushed my head harder into her sex, my nose pressed against her clipped pubic hair. She told me to lick rhythmically against her clitoris. Her legs squeezed against the sides of my head, tight against my temples. My entire face was pressed into her. I breathed in her smell. Her back arched, her hands grasped my head through my hair. She squealed, holding my head against her as I licked and sucked on her open vagina, harder and harder. A gush of fluid shot into my mouth and I drank her salty viscosity.

She laid back and pushed my head away. "Perfect. Good girl."

My life had turned around. Now I had something to live for. I had everything. A newfound exciting femininity and a girlfriend who cared for me. I was able to live through the waitress work and humiliation at Elizabeth's home if I knew I had Elena to look forward to.

What could possibly go wrong?

Chapter 13 - Just a little sting

Elena dropped me off outside Elisabeth's house the next morning, Sunday. I let myself into the house, thoughts of Elena swirled through my head. I loved staying with her, her smell hung in my nose and her taste on my tongue. I sucked on it to taste the remnants of Elena. I closed the door and a lump came to my throat.

Clara came to meet me. Her hands fell to the familiar stance of hands on hips. She splayed her legs apart like a cop on guard duty.

"Upstairs, Patty, now. Get changed into one of your pretty open-fronted skirts. Keep your corset on and your boobs out on display above your corset. High heeled shoes too. Then come down and go into the kitchen." She snarled.

"Now."

Back to normal humiliation. I curtsied and said, "Yes, Mistress." I scooted up the stairs. The contrast with Elena was stark. It didn't pay to hesitate or question Clara, the consequences would have been worse. I reflected on how trained I'd become, despite Elena's claim I still had some rough edges.

After changing, I came back downstairs and into the kitchen. I wore my flowered skirt with the front open and my penis exposed. The corset pinched into my waist. It sat tightly below my enormous exposed boobs and above my pubic triangle. The house was warm but my nipples were erect. I didn't know what had happened during my operation, but my nipples had grown and the areola much wider than before. I hoped

Clara would forget the awful tube cock cage.

I entered the kitchen to see Clara and Elizabeth in discussion with a lady. She had her back to me. Oh no, more humiliation. I saw the lady had long dyed blond hair, similar in colour to my own. My eyes flitted to her pear-shaped bum, the shape outlined in a skin-tight skirt. Here we go again, I thought.

The lady turned. Her red-coloured lips pursed in surprise at my appearance. Oh, is this Patty? How wonderful," she gasped with excitement.

She moved towards me and embraced me. I stood frozen in surprise, not knowing what to do. An over-powering smell of a floral perfume swirled around me. She kissed me on both cheeks and I felt her skirt press against my penis.

Her large boobs clashed against mine and she laughed.

She stood back and looked me up and down. "Wow," she exclaimed. I felt a twitch in my penis at her proximity and friendliness.

"Before we start, Jenny, we have a little process to go through." Elisabeth had her chin cupped in a hand. "As you can see she still gets nasty male urges."

The three ladies gaped at my penis which was erect, despite last night's activities with Elena.

"But it's so cute, Elizabeth." Jenny giggled. "I don't mind. It's nice he, she, finds me attractive." Her eyes flowed over my erection.

Clara pulled on a pair of medical gloves. She was going to milk me. She held a tissue in one hand and pulled at my penis with the other. A wide-eyed Jenny watched in fascination, moving around to get a better view. Clara kept up a refrain of, "Come on, good girl, let it come, good girl." I came into the tissue with a grunt and Clara cleaned me up with the tissue and then with a wet wipe.

Elizabeth passed her the dreaded tube. Clara clasped it around my flaccid penis, trapping the foreskin again. My exposed penis head was on display.

"I'd say we're ready, Jenny." Elizabeth sat down. "The nipples first then her belly button and finally her *little princess*. Let it de-sensitise a bit after cumming. I'm not so cruel." She waited a moment, a wicked smile on her lips. "OK, I'm quite cruel, but do it that way round anyway."

I didn't like the sound of this. Nipples? Belly?

My penis that Elizabeth called *a princess*? Who was this Jenny? My questions were about to be answered.

Jenny produced a pair of tongs and held my left nipple and squeezed it flat. The tongs had a hole through them where they grasped my nipple. She passed a needle through it and my nipple and I screamed at the stinging pain. She hadn't warned me. She withdrew the needle and clipped a half-inch sized ring through the new hole. The stinging soreness persisted.

She gripped the other nipple and repeated the action. She clipped a second ring in and stood back to admire me as I grimaced in stinging pain. She came in close and clipped something onto both rings. She flicked one of them. Little pink tassels. She knelt and then pierced my belly. I squealed and clamped my jaw tight. I watched her put a piece of jewellery through the new hole. It was a fake jewel.

Elisabeth and Clara looked on, admiring my new piercings. I was strangely passive about them, although they were sore. If truth be told, I liked the nipple rings and the belly jewellery although I could have done without the tassels. I knew Elisabeth would want to add something humiliating. I relaxed, assuming Jenny had finished her piercings.

Jenny knelt and faced my penis. "This is going to be uncomfortable, Patty. Close your eyes and I'll try to be quick."

I looked down to see what Jenny was doing. She took the head of my penis in one hand and squeezed it. She had a pair of Clara's medical latex gloves on. It was uncomfortable and I wanted to moan as she opened the slit at the end of my penis. Elisabeth's grim face glared at me and I clamped my mouth shut.

Jenny sprayed something and after a few moments, I lost some feeling in my penis head. She pushed a needle down inside my penis slit. I squealed like a pig as it scratched the inside. I couldn't imagine how bad this would have felt without the numbing spray.

I had no idea what she was trying to do. I found out the next second as she jerked on the needle and it came through the top of my penis head. I screamed, tears welled in my eyes. A metal pin was protruding from the top of my penis. The tears dripped down my cheek.

Jenny withdrew the needle, but the stinging

pain remained. Jenny pushed a thick silver ring, with one end open, into the end of my penis and up through the new hole. She twisted it through then wrapped a piece of gauze around it.

"It should be OK in a day or so," she said.

It didn't feel OK. My penis, nipples and belly had gone from sore to stinging. My penis head throbbed. The silver ring at the end mocked me.

Jenny tweaked the ring into what she considered a better position. Elizabeth and Clara sniggered at each other like two adolescent schoolgirls..

"Put a tassel on the new ring on her *little princess* too, Jenny." Elizabeth giggled from behind her hand.

Jenny clipped on a tassel, the same as those on my nipples. She got up and backed up towards my wife and Clara, the giggling co-conspirator. Jenny folded her arms, inclined her head to one side, and considered her work.

Elizabeth and Clara's giggles continued. "Walk up and down, Patty. I want to see how your tassels swing," said Elizabeth.

I fought back my impulse to run away. There was nowhere to run. My only option to avoid punishment was to walk back and forth while they watched me. I had to allow them their fun. I put one foot forward and walked gingerly towards the end of the kitchen. I spun around and walked back. Elizabeth and Clara collapsed into gales of laughter. I'd never seen Elizabeth let her reserve go so much. She found the sight of me hilarious as I walked up and down, my tassels bobbed side to side from my nipples and penis.

Between her fits of laughter, Elizabeth called out. "Now dance for us. Make your booby and clitty tassels move."

I stopped but I didn't move. This was beyond humiliation, beyond degradation. Elizabeth stopped laughing as if someone had thrown a switch.

"Dance," she ordered.

I jumped at the sudden change in her demeanour. I moved from side to side. My three tassels swung from my nipples and penis ring. A slight soreness persisted. I didn't like the idea of the pain when Jenny's numbing spray wore off.

"Better," she said. "Now a little more."

I increased my movement. The tassels began to loop over and over. Elizabeth howled gales of laughter. I couldn't think of anything she could do worse than this latest humiliation.

At that moment, the doorbell rang. Elisabeth asked Clara to get the door. She told me to carry on dancing as she enjoyed it so much.

Clara returned with Fiona Allerton. Fiona's eyebrows jumped at the sight of me. My tassels swung, my encased penis swayed in time to an imagined tune. Elizabeth and Fiona greeted each other with a kiss on each cheek. Elizabeth waved a hand at me and told me to stop.

"Fiona," she said. "Come to my study. I'm looking forward to hearing what you've come up with for the next stage of Patty's feminisation. Every time you come here it's like opening an unexpected present."

Chapter 14 - On the floor

Elizabeth sent me to my room: She told me I should take a little time to recover from my new piercings. I lay on my bed; my newly tasselled breasts weighed heavily on my chest. Clara didn't come to milk me, my penis was too sore. It was a small comfort.

I wondered how they would tape it up tomorrow for work when it would still be sore. I hoped not to have to go to work with the outline of my ringed penis showing through my thin panties. That might be even worse that the fake vagina.

I stayed in my room all day, dozing with the boredom. Elizabeth didn't allow me a phone or anything to read or watch; there was little else to do but rest.

At around 8 pm, Clara called up to me to join them for dinner. That was odd. Join them for dinner? Up to now, I'd always eaten alone in the kitchen once Elizabeth had finished and I'd cleared up for her. She'd put me on a diet of salad and fish or white meat to keep me slim and feminine.

I suspected dinner with my wife was not going to be a pleasant evening. I descended the stairs, the sound of my heels announced my arrival. I entered the dining room and curtsied without looking. Clara snorted a stifled laugh at seeing my huge boobs and penis with the tassels swinging. The tight corset was my only item of clothing. It sat firmly below my breasts and above my pubic triangle.

Elizabeth pointed to a spot to the side of her chair. "Sit there, girl."

So that was it. Although Elizabeth had invited me to eat with them, I had to sit on the floor. I was to be like a pet. I lowered myself to the floor and Elizabeth patted my head as she chatted with Clara and Fiona. A chrome dog bowl sat on the floor. I saw no knife and fork.

"It's ready, Elizabeth." Margaret, my wife's cook, called out from the kitchen.

Elizabeth placed one elbow on the table. "Go and get the food and serve it to us, Patty."

I pushed myself up with a reluctant effort and went to the kitchen. Margaret was spooning chicken and vegetables onto three large white plates. Her greying hair was tied back in a tight bun on the back of her head. A large back and white apron covered her ample body. Her eyes flashed over my new piercings with the tassels on my breasts and down to my penis. She said nothing but her face twitched a smile. She reached into the oven to retrieve something inside.

I took the plates and clipped back into the dining room. Elizabeth Clara and Fiona watched me in studied silence. I placed the plates in front of each one, curtsying to each as I went. My encased penis pointed out at right angles in the tubular cage. Once I'd served their food, I poured water onto each of their glasses. I stood back and curtsied.

Elisabeth rested her chin on her hands and observed me over her glasses. "Take your little doggy bowl and serve yourself, Patty. Then come back and sit on the floor next to me."

I took the bowl and returned to the kitchen. Margaret looked me up and down again, She never commented on my appearance, but I saw there was something was on her mind. I ignored her and spooned chicken and green beans into my dog bowl then returned to sit on the floor next to Elizabeth.

I picked up a piece of chicken with my fingers and put it in my mouth. Elisabeth pushed a hand to mine to stop me.

"No, Patty, that won't do. Pass me your bowl."

I lifted it to the table. Elisabeth cut my food into little chunks and scrapped half of it into a small plate by the side of her dinner plate. She passed the bowl back to me and told me to put it on the floor. I moved to pick up one of the small pieces of chicken and she slapped my hand.

"No, Patty. Firstly, you served yourself far too much. I need to keep you slim and pretty. I don't want to see you serving yourself so much in future. Do you understand, girly?"

I nodded.

"Secondly, you're to kneel over it and eat with your mouth. Like a little puppy would do."

I stared at her aghast. *Like a little puppy?* I couldn't go on like this. My wife was now treating me like her little pet. I was hungry. I hadn't eaten much and it was late.

I had no choice if I was to eat anything. With a slow heavy movement, I lowered my head towards the dog bowl. My mountainous boobs flopped down over my face. I held my long hair back with one hand and stretched my neck forward to get my face into the bowl. Fiona scraped back her chair and walked from her side of the table to watch my latest degradation. I took a mouthful and chewed. I felt sauce on the end of my nose.

"Good, girl," chirped Fiona as she stroked my head.

She placed a saucer of water next to the bowl. Fiona returned to her seat and they restarted their conversation. They chatted about business matters while I ate with a heavy-hearted humiliation. I finished as much as possible. I slurped at the water through pursed lips.

I sat up when I'd finished, a crick ached in my neck. The weight and size of my breasts caused discomfort, it was as if I had two bags of cement pulling me down. Elizabeth stroked the back of my head, running her fingers through my voluminous hair.

Nothing was worse than how I felt. I sat at Elisabeth's feet, my breasts and penis decorated with piercings and on show for her fun. I had been through so many stages of humiliating misery in my wife's never-ending quest to humiliate me more. Each time I became used to a stage of humiliation, she moved to something new. I wouldn't ask to return to how things had been. I used to be an itinerant male musician and I knew that boat had sailed. Many of my changes were too permanent, too ingrained. My permanent make-up, my breasts. I had to be honest, I felt more female than male and I liked it. But not this latest humiliation. I was a girl, not a pet.

I didn't like was where things were leading now. I was being turned into a bimbo pet for Elizabeth's amusement. Whatever I'd done to her in the past, whatever I'd threatened to do, was finished. I didn't deserve this treatment. Elizabeth knew I was trapped. I had nowhere else to live, no other family or friends and no money.

Elizabeth's single-minded focus on revenge led me to despise her, but I also hated myself for finding her attractive at the same time. I was in awe of her and I was unable to understand why. This was despite how she talked to me, how she treated me. She excited me and I lusted after her. I'd refused to admit that before but it was true. I loved and wanted her with desperation. And I hated her.

The three ladies continued to chat about life as I sat in silence at my wife's feet. I knew not to move without Elizabeth's permission. I was bored, expected to sit quietly at my wife's feet. I looked at her shapely muscular legs, covered in dark fine stockings. She always wore a dress, no more than an inch above the knee. She held herself like a model — her neck and back were as straight as a soldier on parade. Every so often she dropped her hand to stroke my head. This was new. I liked the affection, if that was what it was. It was an upgrade on the spankings and abuse.

I could accept this as my new lifestyle. If I had to be exposed then so be it, I'd get used to it. That would work out eventually in return for not having to think too much about where I'd live and what I'd eat. What I didn't enjoy was the unknown, the new humiliations. At times I wanted to crawl away to my little bedroom and sleep for a hundred years and wake up when it was all over.

Elizabeth bent down to me, breaking my thoughts. "Be a good girl and bring us dessert."

I pushed myself up and scuttled to the kitchen and returned with three dishes of mixed fruit. As I walked in my high heels, the tassels on my nipples swung ticking my breasts.

I curtsied and Elisabeth told me to keep standing. "I want to now begin the next change of your transformation." She clapped her hands in delight. "This will make you so much better than you are now."

She couldn't make things worse, surely. I swayed and the room went dark; the blood seemed to drain from my head to my feet. Why couldn't she leave things as they were? Why did she have to make it worse?

Chapter 15 - Take the pill

Elizabeth placed two pills on the table. One was a small pink oval tablet and the other a tiny white pill. She moved a small plate and tipped a hand-sized portion of seeds from a plastic bag labelled flax seeds. She placed a half-pint glass next to the seeds. She poured what milk from a carton. It read, soy milk. She placed a peach on the table.

Fiona and Clara looked at each other with contented smiles. I had no idea what this was all about, but I guessed it was not good although I couldn't see any harm in anything at that moment.

Elizabeth lifted the tablets. "Take these two little pills and wash them down with the milk."

"What is it, Ms Remington?"

"The cute little pink one is Estradiol and the nice white round one is Anti-androgen. They'll make you better."

"I don't understand, I'm not unwell, Mistress?" This was confusing.

"I didn't say you were unwell, I said the pill will help to make you better as in a better person."

"And how would that be, Ms Remington?" My wife was talking in riddles. What were these pills: Estradiol? Anti-androgen? Slimming pills? I was already slim.

Elizabeth's face hardened and Clara pushed her chair back. My questioning had gone too far. I picked up the tablets, put them both in my mouth, and washed them down with the milk. The milk had a cardboard taste. I had to take a second gulp of milk as one pill caught in my dry throat. A sense of calm fell back around the table as Clara pulled her chair back under the table.

"Good girl, now eat up the nuts and the peach. Think of it as dessert."

That didn't seem to be too difficult, I had a permanent hunger now Elizabeth restricted my diet to keep me slim. I ate on the nuts as the three ladies watched. They were pleased to see me eating, the situation was becoming weirder by the minute. I finished my dessert.

Fiona stood and walked round to me. Her school teacher manner was accentuated by the black-framed square glasses on the end of her nose, Her hair swung from a long ponytail. Her dark grey skirt clung to her tall slim figure. She put a finger under my encased penis, lifted it, and dropped it again disdainfully.

She glanced at Elizabeth then back at me. "Patty. You'll now be on a high-oestrogen diet. Hence the seeds, green beans and soy products. This is not enough alone to improve you so we've put you on the supplements which you'll take twice daily. One is a high dosage version of Estradiol which is oestrogen, the female hormone. The anti-androgen is a testosterone blocker. We don't want you with nasty male hormones. Elizabeth wants to make the changes as soon as possible."

I let her words sink in, high dosage oestrogen? Testosterone blocker? A female hormone? Men had testosterone and women oestrogen. I didn't like this. Everything my wife had done to me so far had changed my appearance only. Underneath I was still male and I clung to that reality. Sure I enjoyed many aspects of my new femininity. I now looked like a girl and I accepted my gender was feminine. But biologically, I was still a male. I wanted that to remain. Now she was about to affect that too and I didn't want it. I had to stop this, whatever the consequences.

"Ms Remington." I fidgeted, frightened at the concept of challenging my wife. Her eyes widened, waiting for the challenge she knew was coming, ready to swat me away. "I don't want to take oestrogen."

I let my words hang in the air. All eyes including mine were on Elizabeth waiting for her response. She seemed to ponder my statement.

"It's not about what you want or not, Patty.

You lost all your rights when you tried to take my money. It's about what I want and what I want is for you to be a pretty bimbo girl. Not a facsimile, as you are now, but a real girl. It's time."

I folded my arms under my giant breasts, forcing them up, showing my bimbo femininity. "I refuse." I stood up and I stamped my foot like a petulant three-year-old, I couldn't help myself. My boobs shook, my penis jiggled.

Elizabeth wasn't fazed by my rebellion. She got up and approached m. Without a warning, she whacked the exposed end of my penis with an open hand. "You will become a real girl if I say so, Patty." She slapped my penis twice more.

I stood firm, taking her slaps. I resolved I was not going to be moved from my position. My resolution felt fragile all the same, what power did I have? None, I depended on my wife for everything. I could refuse to take the tablets and the food, but then what? My resolve flowed away like water down a drain.

Elizabeth lifted my penis with one finger. My foreskin trapped under the metal tube was tight but oddly exciting. My wife's fingertip on the bottom of my sensitive exposed head was tantalising.

"This is a pathetic excuse for a male clitty, but it's too big. The tablets will reduce its size to something more appropriate for a girl." Elisabeth dropped my penis as if it was a piece of dirt. "The oestrogen will remove your nasty male urges and in time we won't have to milk you. That will be better don't you think, Patty?"

I didn't think that would be nice. Not one bit.

"No, Ms Remington. It's not what I want."

"Good," Elisabeth replied. "If you wanted it, I wouldn't do it. Once the oestrogen tablets start to have their effect, you'll change your mind. Either way, I'm not bothered as I want you to be a real girl. That's what you will become."

I had to stop this before my resolve cracked under my wife's pressure. I didn't like conflict and what was so bad about being a girl? It was preferable. I couldn't believe I thought this. Maybe I should accept my wife's ultimatum without fighting back, to accept my fate. If she allowed me to dress more respectfully, being a girl was wonderful. The sexy feelings, the soft beautiful clothing, the feeling of long hair on my shoulders and down my back. My smooth legs on show, sexy and defined.

The end of my manhood was a difficult step to take. It wasn't as if I'd had the feeling to be a girl before Elizabeth had started changing me. I still believed there was a man inside and I didn't want to lose the last piece of my internal jigsaw. In truth, I didn't want to fight with my wife, I wanted her to care for me and provide for me. When I accepted the life she wanted for me, she treated me better. Not as an equal, of course. Even so, I did not want to lose the last vestige of my masculinity. I was in a turmoil of dilemmas. What would Elena think?

Sensing the quandary playing out in my mind, Elizabeth pressed home her advantage. "The only food you'll be getting from now on will be high in oestrogen. Before you eat you'll take the oestrogen tablet and testosterone blocker.

Take the tablets and eat or don't take them and starve."

There was no way out of this. I had become a real girl. Elizabeth the queen had checkmated me again. I had nowhere to go and no one to turn to.

No, that's not true, I did have someone. I had to let Elena know about this.

Chapter 16 - Lifeline

I sat on my bed in the evening, staring at Elena's business card. I'd kept it hidden under my mattress. It was a link to her and I rubbed my finger over her embossed name: Elena Castle.

Elizabeth had dismissed me from the dining room after her speech about me becoming a real girl. I wasn't tired as I'd slept during the long boring day. A cold draught washed around the exposed end of my penis. I held it up by the metal tube, the pink tassel hung against my breast from the ring piercing at the end. A lump came into my throat. Elizabeth wanted my penis to shrivel away.

The evening had been awful. I'd eaten from a dog bowl, drunk water from a saucer, sar at

Elizabeth's feet and made to take female hormones. I couldn't take much more of this.

As much as I now enjoyed the sensations of being a girl, this step was too far. It was too final. I stared hard at Elena's number and an idea came to my mind. I hoped she was a way out of this nightmare. Elena seemed to like me. Hadn't she said it was a shame I had someone else? What if I told Elena I didn't want to be someone else's, I wanted to be hers. That was my escape plan. It was all I had.

The clock by my bed said 10.07 pm. A muffled voice floated up from downstairs. The three ladies were still at the table chatting. Elizabeth had a landline by the side of her bed, if I crept in, it would take only a few minutes to call Elena. Elizabeth was downstairs and likely to be for another hour or so. This idea was a possibility.

I got up. Stealth was difficult in six-inch heels but my wife was not thinking about me now. She was downstairs with her friends relaxing, probably having a cognac or two. I crept out of my room and along the corridor to Elizabeth's bedroom door. I hadn't been in the room since she had made me watch Dan making love to her. I shuddered and put the image to the back of my mind. Calling Elena had to be my focus.

My hand went to the door handle and I twisted it. I pushed on the door and it opened. I pushed it all the way and a loud squeal echoed along the hall. I froze. The voices downstairs stopped. Several moments passed then the mumble of conversation started up again. No footsteps. I was safe, for now. I went in.

The huge bed was as I remembered it the night Dan banged my wife. All the time he had smiled at me. I shuddered at the memory.

I crept to the side of the bed and lifted the phone to my ear. The dial tone purred like a contented cat. I punched in Elena's number, my eyes fixed on the bedroom door. A cold fear swept through me. I heard a ring tone. It rang once, then twice. It rang and rang. No answer. The answering machine clicked in.

"Hello, you have reached Elena... The message stopped and there was a click. "Hello, Elena speaking."

My throat caught. Nothing came out.

"Hello, hello?"

I cleared my throat and whispered. "Hello,

Madam Elena, it's Patricia?"

"Hello, who's speaking? Can you speak up?"

A stair creaked. My shoulders tensed, waiting for another sound. Silence. It was the normal sound of the house. Below, the murmurs of three women's voices hummed.

"Hello, Madam, it's me. Patricia."

A moment of silence on the phone. "Patricia," Elena's voice exploded. "I'm so pleased you called. How are you, my pretty girl?"

My chest zinged at her words. I took a deep breath, my chest rose like dough in an oven then settled back. "I need help."

Elena breathed a slow hiss then said, "I see."

Downstairs a chair scraped across a wooden floor, someone was getting up. A pair of assertive footsteps clipped across the floor below me.

Someone entered the downstairs hall and I stopped breathing. The room became hot.

Elena's voice said, "Hello, are you there still?"

A door squealed open below. It was the downstairs toilet. I breathed out, long and slow.

"I've had enough, "I whispered. "I need to get away from here. Now." I found myself sobbing.

Elena waited a moment as she considered what she was going to say. "What's going on, my poor pretty Patricia?"

All my problems with Elizabeth and her enthusiastic acolytes cascaded out like a torrent of water gushing in a storm. Between my sobs, I explained the story of the hormones and testosterone blockers.

"I see," came the measured response. I'd

expected a much greater outrage from Elena at my story.

"Please help me, Elena. I want to leave this hell and live with you. Please? I was desperate.

A long breath came over the phone. "Are you sure about this, Patty? It's a big step. I don't want a male, I would want you as a feminised and pretty sissy."

I was never more sure about what I wanted. "YES," I screamed too loudly. I listened out for Elizabeth. Nothing. "I want to be your feminised and pretty sissy, Madam Elena."

"Then I'll help you. I'm not able to make it tomorrow, Monday, as I have meetings in Manchester. How about Tuesday, after you finish work? I'll try to get to the pub where you work at 6 pm."

I sighed out deep and long.

"You need to be aware I'm looking for certain things in my life, Patty. You might be what I want. Let's meet in the same café as before and, if you agree to my terms, I'll help you. There has to be something in it for me."

It was a lifeline. Of sorts. I didn't know what her terms would be. It was obvious she liked me but what more did he want from me? Would I be going from the frying pan into a scolding fire? I had nothing to lose. "Thank you, Madam Elena. I will be at the café at 6 pm."

"Patty? Who are you talking to?" Elizabeth's voice screamed up the stairs and into the bedroom.

A shot of polar ice ran through my veins. Elena said something else on the phone and I hung up. I placed the phone receiver back on the cradle as silently as I could. I tip-toed to the bedroom door, thankful Elizabeth had thick carpet on the floor. It muffled my high heels. Elizabeth called out again. "Patty?" The sound of her heels stomping on the wooden stairs echoed like a klaxon.

I was trapped if she came up the stairs at this moment. If I called out from her bedroom, she would notice my voice coming from there. Heat glowed from my cheeks. I had little choice, I had to get out of her bedroom now and get to my room. I could be in a world of trouble and unimaginable punishments.

I swung open the bedroom door and stepped onto the landing.

Chapter 17 - Sissy white lies

The cooler air of the hallway soothed the soreness in my piercing in my exposed penis head. The September temperature had plummeted. It was as if someone had clicked on an autumn switch. My nipples stuck out in the chilly air like projectiles. The tassels flicked across my taut breasts like windscreen wipers in the drizzle.

The stairs flowed down in front of me and twisted round to the hall below. Elizabeth was out of sight around the corner. This meant I was out of her sight too. I glanced back at the bedroom door, it was ajar. Was it closed or opened before I'd gone in? I couldn't remember. Would Elisabeth remember? Yes, she would. Her life was ordered. She always closed doors. And she always remembered everything.

Her footsteps sounded on the stairs; she was coming up. I inched the bedroom door shut with a faint click. I waited for my wife to come up the stairs. She appeared around the corner, her face set on fierce like a bitter winter storm. "Why didn't you answer me, girl? What are you doing skulking about on the landing?"

Elizabeth approached the top stair, she tensed as if poised to attack. She was a lioness about to devour her prey. I had to think of an excuse now. Why was I on the landing at the top of the stairs? It came to me.

"I was asleep. I think I was talking in my sleep and it woke me up. I'm sorry, Ms Remington." How I hated having to address this way.

"Then why are you standing at the top of the stairs, stupid girl?"

She had a point. I rummaged around my mind for a good reason. "I came out to meet you, Ms Remington." I curtsied. In moments of adversity, clarity of mind springs forward.

This took the sting out of her attack. Her face opened not expecting a rational answer. For a sweet short moment, I had the initiative. I knew it was only to be an instant.

"That's good." She waited a moment thinking, not sure if she had missed something.

I'd managed to cover up my little escapade to her bedroom and the phone call.

"Since you're wide awake, you can come downstairs and make coffee before we turn in. I wanted to speak with you tomorrow so we can do it now." She glared, still analysing the situation, thinking she's missing something. She was but I'd removed the clues.

"I know you don't understand why I'm feminising you. Fiona believes I should explain it in easy words for you to digest." She patted the top of my head and ran a hand down one side of my hair, a strange gesture of affection.

She wagged an index finger at me to indicate I should follow her down the stairs. I followed, manoeuvring my corset as I went hoping to get some relief from a small change of position. I didn't.

I stepped down, my metal-encased penis jiggling, my tassels swinging. I went into the kitchen and made fresh coffee in the coffee press.

I took it into the front living room where my wife, Fiona and Clara sat in a low light. Elizabeth only drank fresh coffee served this way.

I poured it into three china cups with dainty saucers and served each lady with a curtsey. I'd done well judging by the approving looks from Elizabeth and Fiona. The three ladies were sitting in a semi-circle. She indicated I sit on the floor at her feet in front of them.

I sat on my legs, my high-heeled feet behind me, my penis pointing up. The corset dug into the pubic mound. The mound was plump thanks to the fat inserted during one of my many feminisation operations. The tassels hung from my huge breasts pert and firm. I pulled at my hair, I wanted to try to use it as a curtain to cover my breasts. My pierced nipples protruded from between strands of hair.

Elizabeth cleared her throat. "Patty." The two ladies on either side of her watched with undisguised anticipation. "Fiona has suggested I speak to you about your process."

Process, I thought? I had other names for what she was doing to me including physical abuse. Much of my feminisation hadn't been so bad but I was not going to tell her that. If only she hadn't been so nasty to get me to where I was now.

"I hadn't seen any point in explaining your process, the reasons why I'm changing you from a male to a female. I didn't believe you'd understand."

I flinched at the directness of what she was saying.

"Fiona told me this process would be much smoother if we explained why you're to become a girl. She feels it would be better if you knew what will be happening to you. I don't believe you have the intelligence to take it in. However, if an explanation smooths your transition then it's an investment worth making. I suppose." Elizabeth flashed a disdainful smirk.

I shuddered. She looked at Fiona, handing the explanation to her. Elizabeth never was one for explaining her actions or reasons. She was uninterested in how others perceived what she did. She sunk back in the armchair, relieved she'd finished with what she considered a waste of time.

"Patricia," Fiona began, using my full feminine name which was a bad sign. "Your feminisation was a punishment for what you tried to do to your wife. Marrying her to take her money. This was money you didn't earn or deserve. It was a nasty thing to do. Once you were on the road to feminisation, Elizabeth saw a new you.

Becoming a female has improved you. We felt you had to be shown humility and to learn about hard work. This is why you work at my gastropub as a waitress. We dress you in very little because your punishment continues."

She waited for her words to sink in. It was true. I had behaved badly. But why shouldn't I have felt entitled to some of her wealth? She had plenty. She could have let me have some and sent me on my way.

Fiona pressed on. "We don't believe you have

learnt your lesson yet; you continue to show sparks of rebellion. You think only of yourself. I can see you have accepted your new femininity and enjoy it. It hasn't escaped our notice how you preen in the mirror."

I flushed red at this comment. I did enjoy my new look. Not the exaggerated bimbo look but my feminine appearance. I liked how I looked. I was attracted to myself. What's wrong with that? The problem was they had turned me into a cartoon version of a girl.

Fiona's eyes bored into me. She knew my mind was racing and she wanted to read my thoughts. I wasn't about to tell her.

Elizabeth cut in. "Fiona, please get on with it, give her the facts and send her to bed. She has to work tomorrow and I want her to look extra feminised and even more of a bimbo tomorrow." Elizabeth was becoming bored with spending time explaining her actions.

Fiona continued. "The endpoint is that we have decided that you are to become a real girl, not a pretend version. Now you've started on the hormones, there will be a great change in you. Things will accelerate from there. We're reaching the final stages of your transformation. There will be one more process and then you'll be a real girl. There will be no discussion or turning back."

Elizabeth tapped her foot and leant forward. "To get to the point. You can either drag your heels and become a real girl or accept it, enjoy the journey, and become a girl. However you decide to react, you will become a girl. Permanently. There will be nothing male remaining. Nothing. I'm removing everything male from you."

I rocked on my legs. Elizabeth was as blunt as ever.

"Any questions, Patricia?" Fiona took a sip of coffee as if what she'd said was a comment about the weather.

I had a ton of questions but one burnt into me like a hot poker. "What exactly does Ms Remington mean by removing everything male?" My penis tingled in rebellion.

Elisabeth snorted, "Stupid girl."

Fiona put down her coffee cup and looked up. "The hormones will reduce the size of your clitty, which is excellent news. You're about five inches now and I guess it will cease to function much and you'll be around an inch long in time."

"An inch?" I sat up and blurted out. Panic flew through every part of me. I had accepted and enjoyed my feminisation, much to the annoyance of my wife. This was on the implicit understanding my penis remained intact and functioning. Or so I had thought. Implicit, that was the issue. This was still a step too far. Fiona's speech and Elizabeth's message about accepting it was not going to happen as far as I was concerned.

"Patricia, I know this is a shock to you but you can't be a girl with a functioning five-inch male part? It's not right." She looked at me as if this was natural logic. "Once it's not functioning, we'll remove it and your ugly balls have it remodelled into a pretty vagina."

"But, but, Mistress Fiona, I promise to be a

good girl and let you do anything. Please let me keep my male bits." My desperation was sweating out of me.

The three ladies looked at each other. Fiona looked back and chuckled as if unable to believe what I'd said. "Don't be ridiculous."

Elizabeth stood, exasperated. "Enough. I told you she wouldn't understand. She's too stupid." She looked down at me and pointed at my tubed penis. "You can't be a proper girl and have that or those nasty balls behind it. Look at them, they're disgusting. You look like a freak. They're going. Chopped off and thrown away." She stomped out of the room. Her footsteps clomped up the stairs. A door slammed moments later.

I gasped. "Mistress Fiona? Not my penis and balls."

Fiona and Clara looked at each other then back at me. Fiona raised her eyebrows and shrugged her shoulders.

Being feminised was one thing. Things had taken a turn for the worse. I hadn't thought that possible.

Chapter 18 - Cuckolded and pegged

I sat on the dining room floor at Elisabeth's feet. Clara had pulled my corset a notch tighter causing my firm breasts to push out even further. Elizabeth grumbled about getting me to a 22-inch waist. It was taking too long.

My pretty chiffon skirt draped on the floor behind me. The open front fell away on either side of my metal tube encased penis. The chrome dog bowl was in front of me. It was full of oestrogen packed seeds, chickpeas and various green vegetables. I ate them without enthusiasm otherwise I'd go hungry. I dipped my head into the bowl and fed.

I told myself it won't be long until I escaped. I had Elena.

The obnoxious smarmy self-satisfied dinner guest, Dan, sat opposite grinning.

I'd endured another full day as a waitress at the pub. There was one more day to go and my ordeal would be over. I'd meet Elena tomorrow evening and agree to anything she asked. I'd remain a pretty girl for her without the humiliation. That's what I was now, a pretty girl. There would be no further changes and she would treat me a lot better than my wife.

I wished Elena could save me now. I wanted her to take me in and rescue me from my evil wife and her cohorts. I loved my femininity, I was not going to let that go. I loved my pretty looks and the envious looks. And the lusting looks. I was attractive. My great looks had transferred from masculinity to femininity with ease. They were not going to take my penis away. Why couldn't I be a girl with something extra?

With dinner finished, Elizabeth and Dan focused on each other. I watched them through my long false eyelashes as they stroked each other's hands. They kissed. They had forgotten me, or at least consigned me to the back of their memories in the way you do a servant.

I heard Margaret leave, the dinner completed. Clara had left the room. I guessed she had gone to her room in the attic extension.

I looked around, not knowing what to do with myself. I wasn't allowed to leave without my wife's permission and I had nothing to do but to watch and listen to my wife flirting with her lover. I guessed that was the point of me being there. Resentment burned in my gut. I still had some male pride buried inside me.

She had humiliated and cuckolded me with Dan, but I found I was still drawn towards her. There was a fascination in what she was doing to me, I was like a moth to a flame and I was being burnt. Her dismissive attitude was exciting and I hated myself for feeling like this. As they whispered into each others' ears and giggled, excitement built at seeing them openly cuckolding me. I looked away, disgusted at my thoughts and feelings.

I heard a chair slide back. I looked up to see Dan standing. He put his hand out and Elizabeth stood and took it. They walked past me and I hoped they would leave me there. Their body language pointed to only one outcome for tonight. I hated Dan. I hated his perfect hair and his perfect smile. I hated his expensive suit, his open-necked and tailored shirt. Worse still, I hated he had my wife and I didn't. I loved it too.

They walked to the door hand in hand, eye to eye. Elizabeth stopped. "Patty, follow us to the living room. I want you to see something." She hunched her shoulders and sniggered through her hand.

They waited by the door. I got up and Dan's eyes dropped to my penis and then settled on my breasts. He threw me his 1,000-watt smarmy smile but his eyes were cold.

I followed them to the living room. Elizabeth told me to sit on the floor. They kissed with passion as if I wasn't there. Their hands fell over each others' bodies. I tried to look away, but the intensity of their swirling passion pulled me back in. Elizabeth dropped to her knees, her eyes on his bulging trouser front. She fought with Dan's belt buckle then his trouser buttons. She undid them in a frenzy. Her eyes flicked to me then back to Dan's flies. Her lips were set in a thin taunting smile.

She pulled Dan's trousers down with a sharp tug. He stood in tight designer underpants, his erection pushed out the front. Elizabeth gasped and his smile broadened. His glistening white teeth shone like a torch under the lamplight. She bit gently on his manhood through the underpants. I looked down at the floor, deflated.

Elizabeth ripped his underpants down to his ankles with a jerk. Dan's monstrous erection sprung up to face her. It was impossible to tear my eyes away. Dan stepped out of his crumpled trousers and underpants.

Elisabeth licked around the head of his giant erect penis. Her long tongue slurped against the end. She pursed her lips around it and sunk her mouth over it. I gasped at how she swallowed it to the end of his shaft. How was that possible? She withdrew, kissed the end of Dan's throbbing erection and looked across at me with a sneer.

"Be a good girl and fold up Dan's trousers and underpants for him, Patty." Elizabeth took a moment before descending onto her lover's erection again. Her luscious mouth wrapped around it like a suction pad. I wished it was my penis she was gorging on.

I watched and wondered, how did she enjoy sucking a penis that big? She'd never sucked on my penis, even when we first married. I gazed down at my caged five inches with regret.

I got up and folded Dan's trousers and underpants. I placed them on a chair while my wife sucked and slurped on Dan's enormous shaft. Resentment burned in me and I fought against watching them from the corner of my eyes. She was making a good show of enjoying the size. It had to be uncomfortable in her mouth and throat, it was too big. Surely? She had to be pretending to annoy me. Her forefinger pointed for me to sit again whilst she had Dan's penis in her mouth.

She withdrew from the huge erection. Elizabeth stood and shimmied out of her panties under her dress. "Watch and learn, Patty," she said as she turned her back to Dan and bent over. "As a girl, this is what you'll be doing.

Different hole, the same result."

Dan pushed my wife's dress up and moved in. His huge erection disappeared inside her, a permanent grin pasted on his face. Elizabeth gasped an, "Oooh."

My eyes watered. How had she taken nine inches of solid penis? I wanted my erection inside her, not Dan's. I couldn't tear my horrified eyes from the unfolding scene. They moved back and forth in a slow tango that became faster and faster. They panted and sweated, their bodies thrust into each other.

Elizabeth called out, "More, my darling, deeper, harder"

Deeper? She already had too much inside her. Their bodies jerked together, their dance slowed and stopped. They fell back on the floor.

Elizabeth smoothed down her dress. Dan slumped on a chair, some of his discharge oozed from his limp expended penis. It hung between his legs, long and fat, like a huge sausage. His eyes fell on me, his grin re-energised. I jerked my eyes away.

"Your turn, Patty."

Elizabeth's flushed face was the only sign that anything had happened. Dan's penis size hadn't caused her any problems after all.

"I said, it's your turn now, Patty. "

What did she mean, my turn? She called Clara as Dan slipped his trousers back on. They sat together on the sofa facing me. Dan's put his arm around Elisabeth's shoulder and they shuffled up together as if they were about to watch a film. The door squealed open behind me and Clara's heavy footsteps sounded.

"Bend over, girly." Elizabeth swirled a hand in the air.

I bent. Clara came into view through my legs and I tried to stand again. Elizabeth jumped up and pushed my head down.

Clara had a black leather belt strapped around her waist over the top of her grey trousers. A huge life-like plastic cock stuck out from the front. It was almost as large as Dan's erection.

I had little time to think about the situation. She pushed the strap-on cock hard against my bum hole. I squealed like a pig at the shock. She slid it in an inch with a single thrust of her hips.

I screamed. Clara pushed it halfway. My eyes watered, I wasn't sure if was in pain or pleasure.

She shoved further in without affection, each thrust caused me to howl. It wasn't comfortable but not as terrible as I expected.

Clara slid her strap-on cock in and out of me as Elisabeth and Dan watched. It became smoother and I relaxed as waves of pleasure swept through me. I held back so Elizabeth didn't know the experience was becoming wonderful.

If only my wife and Dan weren't watching. Tuesday evening with Elena couldn't come fast enough.

Chapter 19 - He's such a pretty girl

I waited in the café as I'd agreed with Elena on Tuesday evening. It had been the longest wait I could remember. I fidgeted on the seat impatience and because my bum was sore from Clara pegging me.

I twiddled my fingers and tapped on the tabletop with my talon-like pink nails. I wouldn't be playing the guitar with these nails any time soon. I put a hand on my knee to stop tapping my heel on the floor.

Elizabeth had overseen my clothing this morning. It had been a warm morning and Elizabeth had said she wanted to step up my humiliation another notch or two. How was that even possible? I found out it was.

She put me in a tiny luminous yellow dress. I had a halter-neck top with an open back. The halter neck straps looped around my neck and were little more than one inch wide over my nipples. I had no bra; my breasts were firm despite their size. The silicon inside was high quality.

The rings through my nipples showed through the thin material on the narrow straps. I was all but topless. The halter straps attached to a gathered waistband below my breasts. The dress flared out three inches from my high skinny waist in small pleats. My panties were on full display. To call this a dress was an exaggeration. It was little more than two thin straps attached to a piece of cloth above my panties.

Clara had strapped up my penis with tape and pushed my balls inside me. The vagina shaped mould showed a perfect camel toe outline.

Elizabeth had made me wear white fishnet stockings. I wore them with a white lace suspender belt. My stocking tops and suspender straps showed.

I wore new shoes — patent white leather sandals clamped with the tiny heart-shaped padlocks. I played with my enormous loop earrings. I felt like a porn movie star, *Patty Does London.*

This was no movie. I was sitting in a café in a west London suburb in broad daylight experiencing the giggles and stares of everyone who saw me.

It was 5.35 pm and Elena was five minutes late. I desperately wanted her to arrive so I didn't have to endure my humiliation alone. I fiddled with my halter strap. It dug into the ringed nipples. Two young men and three women stared at me in disbelief from the next table. I fought with the strap to find some comfort without exposing a pierced nipple.

I glanced again at my slim female watch on my skinny wrist. 5.40 pm. Elena was ten minutes late. This didn't look good. Maybe she'd decided not to get involved? I hunched into my seat, hoping people would tire of staring at me. I sipped on a small cup of coffee. My pink nails were stark against the white china

Elizabeth didn't allow me to have a phone so Elena couldn't contact me. I could do nothing but read the menu card and watch the world pass by outside. And blank out the looks.

Time clicked on to 5.45 pm. It seemed Elena wasn't coming. Fifteen minutes was too late. I didn't know what she could do for me but there was no one else to turn to. She had to help me. I needed her.

The door swung open. Elena strode in and scanned the room. Her eyes locked on me; for a moment she didn't register. It was the new dress. Or more accurately, the vestiges of a dress since all she could see was a near-naked blond bimbo wearing two thin straps over giant boobs.

Her eyes lit up and she came over. She slipped in next to me. Her light-grey business suit was a model of decorum against my bright canary-yellow straps and little frill of a dress. She wore her white blouse done up to the neck. My dress was almost non-existent. She kissed my cheek, her fruity perfume smelled fresh and clean.

"Wow," she said, her eyes moved all over me. They landed for a few moments on my breasts before moving to my stocking tops. Her hand brushed along the lace.

I was anxious to find out if she could help me escape from Elizabeth.

"Hello, Madam Elena."

It felt odd to refer to her so formally as she was not formal or distant. She treated me as a friend apart from her insistence on me calling her Madam.

"I'm so pleased you came, I was worried you wouldn't come. I wondered if you'd changed you're mind. I didn't know how to contact you." I stopped myself from blabbering further.

"Before we start, Patricia, I want you to fetch me a green tea. I'm gasping for a drink, I had to rush from a business meeting to get here."

I looked at her in horror. The customers in the coffee bar had lost interest in me once she arrived and now I'd have to parade to the bar in full view. Elena seemed not to notice and passed me a £20 note. "Here you are, get yourself something too."

I didn't take it and looked at her hoping she'd realise how humiliating it was to parade up to the shop counter again.

Her slight smile faded at my hesitancy. "Patricia dear, if you want my help, you're going to have to do what I ask you to do."

She spoke in a friendly manner but the implication was clear. This was a woman I had to obey, even if she framed her orders in a more pleasant way than Elizabeth's.

I took the £20 note and pushed back the chair. I fluffed down my dress to no effect and straightened the straps over my nipples. I looked at the floor and marched to the bar as if I was the most confident girl in the world. Inside I shook. I'd spent the entire day dressed this way and I'd have to endure more.

I ordered Elena's tea and another coffee for me. I waited at the end of the bar for the barista to make our drinks. I caught Elena smiling up at me before returning to her phone. My eyes went to the sexy girl in the wall mirror behind the bar.

The girl wore a tiny yellow dress and had a

mountain of blond hair Her eyelashes flicked like black sails and she had beautiful breasts spilling out from thin straps. I gulped hard. It was me. My eyes locked on my reflection. I was a parody of my own fantasy. Slim, sexy and female. I wanted to stare at this incredible sexy creature in the mirror.

"Your drinks, miss."

The barista's deep voice pulled me back to reality. I picked up the two cups, the barista's eyes fixed on my chest, straining behind the two thin straps. I spun around, the tiny material of my skirt swished against the top of my bum like a ballet dancer's tutu. Eyes burned into me again. The hubbub of background noise increased as I marched back towards Elena. She watched me and an amused look twinkled in her eye.

I sat down. Elena reached out to one of my breasts and tucked a finger under the halter-neck strap. It had moved to one side, exposing an erect proud nipple and ring. Elena flicked my nipple back under the strap.

She sipped her drink and leant into my personal space. She stroked my face with a forefinger. "You're such a pretty girl. Tell me all about your new problem. And your new piercings." Her eyes gleamed.

I downloaded everything. I spoke without break for fifteen minutes. I told her about the hormones and oestrogen-rich food. I told her Elizabeth wanted to make my penis shrink to one inch. And that she wanted to remove my penis and balls once they no longer worked.

Elena listened without interruption. Occasionally she touched my hand. Under the strong tape, my penis tried in vain to flick into life. I finished speaking, mentally drained. I felt better.

Elena took my hand. "Do you like being a girl?"

Her question surprised me. I had expected her to sympathise with me, ask about the hormones, to tell me my wife was a beast. Instead, she asked a question about whether I liked my new gender or not. I look to the ceiling for inspiration. I wasn't sure what I wanted. I loved my femininity. I didn't want to go back to the man I'd been. On the other hand, I didn't want Elizabeth to shrink my penis with hormones. Or worse. I was mixed up, confused.

"Do you have to think about it, Patty? I'd have hoped you had made your mind up by now. Are you going to disappoint me?" Elena's face creased.

I had to give her the answer she wanted, that way she would help me to escape the clutches of my evil wife. Elena liked me feminised. Hell, I liked being feminine. I didn't like how I looked like a fantasy prostitute though. My best approach was to tell Elena the truth and not attempt to second guess what she was looking for.

"Madam Elena, I enjoy my new femininity. I'm not happy with my wife making me dress this way. I feel exposed. I want to wear a pretty dress to cover my panties and a top that doesn't show off my breasts so openly. I want to look like a normal girl, but I don't want to lose my male bits. I'm confused. It's as if I want both sides of me."

Elena observed me for a moment. Her face broke into a wide smile. "Excellent. Perfect answer. I knew you were what I was looking for, despite your somewhat exaggerated dress sense. I'm looking for a submissive feminised male. I would want you to remain at my home and be my housewife." She thought for a moment. "No, more of a housemaid. I'd expect you to clean my house daily, to prepare my dinners and serve them. I want to play with you whenever I feel like it. I'll have some of my female friends around and you'll serve them too."

This sounded wonderful.

"You'll be feminised and pretty at all times

for me. I have no interest in you if you want to return to masculinity. You'll keep your little bits and I don't want you to take hormones. I'd like you to have a working male clitty as I find this is an excellent way to control feminised men. If this is acceptable, I'll take you in on a trial basis."

I'd been holding my breath and I released in a long slow hiss of relief. "Yes, yes that is wonderful Madam, I'm so happy, Madam." Then the realisation hit me. It wouldn't be so simple. Elizabeth stood in the way of my salvation. "So what now? I don't think Elizabeth will let me go, she's enjoying my humiliation too much."

Elena wasn't concerned about this. "Go home tonight, Patty, and pretend all is normal and do what your wife tells you. I'll get my house ready for you and buy some better clothing and underwear for you. After work tomorrow, I'll wait here with my car and we'll go to my home. I live a few miles outside London so we are unlikely to ever bump into Elizabeth again. Besides, you'll be working in my hone daily. You'll be free of her. But, I want you to act normal tonight."

This sounded wonderful. It was difficult to take it in. I was to escape from my horrid wife and live with the caring wonderful Madam Elena. She promised a lifestyle where I'd have a strong woman ruling over me. This time, it would be one who cared about me.

We said goodnight. I left for Elizabeth's house for what I hoped would be the last time. I'd gone through a long journey, an incredible transition, and I was going to come out out the other side as a better person. A new person. A girl.

My head was light and my body floated as I returned home. By tomorrow evening, my nightmare would be over. I'd be with my love, Madam Elena. My throat ached, I wanted to cry in relief, love and joy. Elation flowed through me.

This was too good to be true.

Chapter 20 - Travel plans

A full moon shone in a clear dark sky. The streetlight outside the front gate threw an eerie amber light across the front porch. I let myself in the front door. I wiped the smile from my face from the memory of Elena. I was to act normally, that's what Elena had said. A smile would be out of place. It had been a long time since Elizabeth had seen me smile.

I closed the door behind me. Scattered about the entrance hall were six suitcases. Locked, tagged and ready to go.

Clara came out from the kitchen. Her wide black trousers flapping around her ankles like two flags on stout poles. She bustled around the cases without speaking to me and ignored my curtsey.

Elizabeth burst into the hallway, two passports in hand. "Oh, there you are. Finally. Take our cases out to the drive, the taxi will be here in a moment. I wondered where you'd got to. I was about to call that friend of yours." Elizabeth stopped and folded her arms.

I curtsied and asked her where we were going.

"I'll explain on the way to the airport," she said.

"Airport? But I can't, "I spluttered. "I have a…," I stopped myself. This was going wrong. My escape plans had turned to ashes.

"You have what, girly? A job to go to? Don't worry, I've discussed it with Fiona and you will go back to work at the pub when we get back from Brazil."

The floor seemed to rise up towards me and the walls closed in. A black curtain fell over my eyes. I woke a few minutes later with cold water dripping on my face. Elizabeth held up a pink blouse, tan hold-up stockings and a short flowery skirt. "Put these on. They will be a little more appropriate for travelling in."

I pushed myself back onto my feet, shaking. I shook my head. I took the clothes from Elizabeth and changed in the hall. The skirt was mid-thigh so I didn't need to be asked twice. It was good to have my panties covered. The skirt hung lightly against my thighs and made me feel sexy. I buttoned the blouse up to my neck. Elizabeth re-locked my shoes back on after I had put on the hold-up stockings.

My joy at wearing pretty clothing was squashed by the revelation we were about to fly out of the country. Away from Elena, away from my future. Elizabeth had a very different future planned for me. I had no idea what. Maybe it was nothing more than a holiday. If it was, I wanted no part of it. I wanted Elena.

Elizabeth tutted in a good-natured way as she unbuttoned my blouse to show my cleavage. She stood back and inspected me for a moment, nodded, and swept into the next room. I carried the bags outside as she'd asked.

As I plonked the cases down, a silver people carrier swung into the driveway and crunched on the gravel. It stopped with a slide and a squeal of brakes. The driver jumped out and stared at me with a large smile plastered across his leering face.

"Let me help you with those, miss," he said.

He took the bags from my grip his eyes darting all over my legs and huge cleavage. He put the cases in the rear of the vehicle. Perspiration dripped down my neck despite the fresh evening air. I had to find a way to get a message to Elena. This was a disaster. She'd think I'd changed my mind.

I went back into the house and tried to think. Elizabeth was old fashioned and had a landline in the living room. Elizabeth and Clara buzzed around the hall like two bees in a flower meadow. I hoped the preparations distracted them. I slipped into the living room and clicked the door shut. My legs wobbled, my head swam. A headache throbbed above my eyes.

I picked up the phone and started to dial Elena's mobile phone. My fingers pressed two buttons together. I hung up and tried again. I told myself to calm down. I took a long deep breath.

"Patty, Patty. Where are you?" Elizabeth called from the hall.

I started to tap in Elena's number again. 077...I stopped. Did her number start 07751 or 07715? My mind froze. Think, I said to myself.

"Patty." Louder now. More urgent.

Sweat rolled down my neck. I had to get a message to Elena. I had seconds to make the call, my wife and Clara were outside the door. I had to guess. One shot. I tapped it in. 07715 then the rest of the number. It rang. The door handle went down. It opened a crack.

"Patty, are you in there? I'm going to punish you if you don't answer.

A second ring. A click. A sleepy female voice. "Hello?"

The door swung open a little more and Clara stepped in. I had to garble my message quick. "Elena it's me. Elizabeth is taking me away tonight. I'll call you when I can."

"Who's that? The voice was now awake: stern and enquiring. It wasn't Elena. "You've got the wrong number." They hung up.

I'd chosen the wrong phone number option. Clara stomped over and snatched the phone away from my hand. She slapped my cheek hard, hung up the phone and dragged me outside by an arm.

Elizabeth sat in the front of the vehicle and

Clara got into the back with me. We set off. Soon we were in heavy evening traffic on a busy dual carriageway. All signs pointed towards London Heathrow Airport. Elizabeth swung her head around from the front seat. She looked me up and down, her eyes narrowed hard. She had dashed my dreams of escape with her relentless persecution.

I'd been unable to tell Elena that Elizabeth had forced me to leave. She would think I'd got cold feet and she'd find someone else. She was wonderful. I'd found what I wanted, only for my wife to rip it away. I felt a rising panic in my chest. I knew Elena could find another girl like me, I was sure there would be many willing males for someone like her.

I caught Elizabeth watching me, my face

giving away the hysteria swirling inside me. A familiar condescending smirk slid across her lips.

"What's going on, Ms Remington, "I asked. "Why are we going to the airport?" The panic rose in my voice.

"We're going to Brazil. They have a fantastic plastic surgery business and I know of a doctor there who won't ask any questions."

Her face displayed triumph. Every victory against me gave her intense pleasure.

"Fiona told me it might take months or even years for the hormones to kick in and shrink your little thingy. I can't wait that long, so we're going to Brazil to get it cut off and a pretty vagina built in its place. Isn't that wonderful, Patty? You're to get a proper vagina like a real girl. I can then wait for the hormonal changes to finalise the rest of your feminisation. A pretty girl can't have a male penis and balls, it's not right."

Elizabeth swung back around, conversation finished. My throat closed up as my mouth went dry. My neck seemed to swell, I couldn't breathe. I cleared my throat and licked my dry lips.

"But, Ms Remington, I don't want it cut off." I had to plead. "I promise to be a good girl, I'll do anything you want."

I enjoyed my femininity and I didn't want to go back to what I used to be but this was too much, too drastic.

Elizabeth turned again. "Nonsense, Patty. You just need a little push. Once it's done you'll be very happy, like with your breasts. You like them, don't you? Stop whining."

Elizabeth passed the two passports to Clara next to me. Clara opened one on the back page. She held it to my face. Patricia Candy Tiffany Remington. What? My eyes fell on the face photo. It was me. How had she done that? I looked closer. Sex. Female. Elizabeth had somehow got a passport for me as a girl.

"I decided Candy and Tiffany were cute middle names. I wish I'd thought of them before." The back of Elizabeth's mane of dark hair mocked me.

Chapter 21 - Departure time

An hour later, we arrived at the airport departure terminal. I racked my mind to think of a way to call Elena before we took off, to let her know I was being taken away. I was desperate as Elizabeth and Clara whisked me through check-in, security and the departure lounge. We waited for the flight to Sao Paulo. This was a nightmare. I couldn't sit still. Elizabeth and Clara stayed on either side of me, like my very own Praetorian Guard. Their escort duties were not for my personal security but to ensure I did what my wife wanted.

We entered the plane and a pretty air hostess greeted us at the door. Clara gave me my boarding card. I looked at it then at her.

"We're going into business class. You have an economy seat at the back. We'll see you in twelve hours."

Clara and my wife spun off towards the front of the plane. I remained there in shock. I thought about running back.

"This way, Madam." The young hostess guided me in the other direction as a bad-tempered queue formed behind me. People mumbled complaints at my delay.

"Get a move on lady." A woman's voice called out before saying to her husband, "She looks like a prostitute."

I looked behind me. There was nowhere to run, the corridor behind me was full of passengers waiting to board. I strode along the plane aisle and found my seat next to a window. I settled in and brushed my skirt flat against my thighs.

My mind raced as the seats filled. I needed to think. My only thought was I had to contact Elena, she'd know what to do. A man slid in the seat next to me, he was texting on a mobile phone as he settled down. He nodded a greeting and a leer shot into his eyes. He locked onto my breasts. I cringed. He put his phone down on his lap, his man-spread legs were tight against mine. I held my position but he didn't give way. Instead, he raised a leg on one toe and let it down again rubbing against my leg.

I stared at him and he looked back and raised an eyebrow. An idea hit me.

"Hello, nice to meet you," I cooed in my best little girl voice. I put my head to one side in what

I thought might be a suggestive manner. This might be a challenging flight, I thought.

"Hello, pretty lady." He grinned wide.

He hadn't seen through me. His eyes were planted on my large cleavage rather than my face.

I made my move. "Could I borrow your mobile phone, sir? For a few moments? I left mine at home and I desperately need to call my sister and let her know I'm OK. Please?"

He grinned and said, "Sure, cutie."

He passed the phone over. I reached for it then he snatched it away. "My name is Pete. I'll let you borrow my phone if you tell me your name and agree to let me take you for dinner in Sao Paulo. You're one hot chick."

I swallowed hard. This was going to be a

difficult journey. His hand dropped to my bare leg above my knee. He stroked my thigh with his fingertips and I fought against the disgust showing across my face. He wasn't looking at my face and he missed my grimace.

"Of course, how lovely," I lied. "My name is Patty." I held my hand out, my fingers loose.

He slapped his phone into my palm and I shuddered at his light touches against my knee.

I punched in Elena's number. This time my mind was clear despite my desperation. I remembered her number as I wiped my forehead. I didn't know what she could do but I trusted her to think of something. A ringing sounded. A second ring then, "Hello? Elena Castle." Thank God I thought.

"Elena."

The man next to me pretended to read the in-flight magazine.

"Is that you, Patty?"

"Yes, Elena."

"Patty, I told you to call me Madam."

"Elena, I don't have much time. I'm on a borrowed phone."

"Patty, I'm very pleased to hear from you, but I'm not going to listen until you use my title."

I glanced at the man next to me.

"I'm waiting, Patty." Elena's voice barked from the receiver.

"Madam." I started. Pete's head swung round to look straight at me. His forehead creased.

"Much better. Now. What can I do for you, Patty?"

"Madam. Elizabeth is taking me…"

"Excuse me, madam." A sharp female tone cut across me. A hostess was leaning over towards me. "Mobile phones off please."

I gasped in desperation. "I'm sorry I need to give my friend this message."

"Now," ordered the hostess.

"I won't be a minute, I promise."

A tinny voice sounded in my ear. "What's going on, Patty? Where are you?"

"We're going to take off shortly, if you don't turn the phone off, madam, I'll eject you from the plane immediately."

That was exactly what I wanted. A bubble of excitement sprung up. An opportunity. I stared her down, daring her. I wanted her to eject me. Pete snatched the phone from my grasp. A disconnected voice sounded, "Patty what...?" He stabbed the red button and Elena's lifeline fell away.

"Thank you, sir." The hostess stood straight, glared at me and marched off.

Pete tucked the phone into an inner jacket pocket. "You're a feisty one, Patty. I like that in a girl." His hand fell to my knee. I brushed it away. This was going to be a long flight.

Chapter 22 – Intimate inspections

I lay back on the metal-framed trolley bed, my legs wide apart. She inspected my pierced penis and balls with latex-gloved hands and lit by a torch on her head. Her eyebrows raised a fraction at the sight of the Prince Albert ring through my penis. It's a fleeting break in her professional demeanour. My skirt and panties were slung on a chair in the corner of the white-walled room. I had my six-inch heels on, Elizabeth claimed she'd forgotten the key. Elizabeth never forgot anything.

An air conditioning unit hummed from above a large aluminium-framed window. I was cold: the chilled air was set too low for comfort. A muffled roar permeated the room from outside.

The contiguous metal snake of Sao Paulo traffic ground past the private hospital ten floors below us. The spring sunlight cut into the room like a laser beam. Outside the temperature edged towards a balmy 23C / 74F.

Clara and Elizabeth paced the room, arms folded. The plastic surgeon hummed as she continued her investigation. Once satisfied, she got up. She went to a desk on the other side of the office and sat. I remained on the hospital trolley, legs akimbo.

She looked up from her papers, above a pair of narrow glasses. "You may get dressed now, miss." The hint of an accent but otherwise, her English was perfectly formed.

I slid off the trolley bed and pulled on my panties and skirt with relief. Elizabeth had exposed me to many women but I never got over the degradation of my penis being examined by a dispassionate, fully-clothed woman.

Elizabeth and Clara waited, watching the plastic surgeon. We had landed in Sao Paulo yesterday. I was jet-lagged and disorientated from the flight and time difference. Clara also looked as if she need to rest. Elizabeth was her usual self, immaculate, bustling around and looking as if she'd had a perfect night's sleep.

The plastic surgeon was a moody looking olive-skinned lady in her fifties. Her raven-black hair was flecked with grey, as if she had paint streaks splashed over her head. She removed her glasses and let them hang from her neck on a slim silver chain. She removed her head torch and flicked off her latex gloves, dropping them in the bin as if they carried a contagious disease.

"So, Ms Remington. All seems fine and I will operate in two days," she said.

Elizabeth's eyes narrowed. "Why do we have to wait two days, Dr Lopez? I'm ready for Patty's operation now."

Dr Lopez fiddled with her glasses and bit her lips. "It takes that long for the preparations and I have another patient to operate on before Patricia." She put her glasses back on and began to write some notes, disinterested in my wife's protestations. It was good to see someone stand up to my wife's bullying.

"I'll pay more to have Patricia brought forward. Tomorrow? This afternoon? How much?"

"It's not a question of money, Ms Remington.

I've already brought Patricia's procedure forward. Two days is what it is."

Elizabeth gave a tiny nod of agreement. She'd given in and I marvelled that Elizabeth had met her match. I'd never seen that before. At the same time, I was in a state of denial. This was not happening, was it? I was floating along with Elizabeth's plan hoping something would come up. Was she going to have my penis and balls removed and sculptured into a vagina? If I had any doubt, Dr Lopez flipped her laptop screen around. A diagram of a female vagina filled the screen.

"This is the design I'll be giving Patricia."

Horror coursed through my body. My self-denial was blown away like a feather in a hurricane. Elizabeth was going to do this to me.

"Can't you make her labia bigger, fatter? More obvious? I want the outline of her lips to show through her panties." Elizabeth scrutinised the picture.

Dr Lopez tapped on some keys and the diagram changed to the fatter labia Elizabeth had suggested.

She stood back and finger on her chin. "Yes, perfect, Dr Lopez."

This was not perfect at all. "Excuse me," I said.

Three heads turned towards me, each one looking as if they had forgotten I was there in the room.

"What is it, stupid girl? Can't you see we're busy?" Elizabeth's snappy response betrayed her disguised tiredness.

"I don't want a vagina. I want..."

"Nonsense. You'll love it once you get it." Elizabeth waved my protest away with a dismissive hand wave. "Imagine, you will be able to take a nice hard male cock in your vagina. You'll thank me."

Dr Lopez's attention remained on the screen, uninterested in my complaint. The $20,000 in cash she was charging Elizabeth for my operation was her clear priority. I bit my tongue to avoid the punishment that would ensue if I argued. My mind buzzed with new plans for escape while they discussed the finer points of my proposed operation. This was one thing I was going to fight. I was on my own against them. There would be no Elena to sweep in and rescue me now. Elizabeth had snatched that option from my grasp.

Elizabeth and Clara had stayed with me every moment since we'd arrived. Elizabeth had her own hotel room but Clara was rooming with me. That gave me a chance. When she showered, I would take the opportunity to run out of the room and escape. I had to find a way to remove my six-inch heels. There was no way I could outrun anyone in towering stiletto heels. The locks on my shoes were tiny. The more I thought about it, the more I was sure I could pick them. The padlocks looked weak. Maybe all they would need is a pin or a paperclip to unpick them.

Dr Lopez's desk was tidy and clear except for a paper document on the edge. The three ladies huddled around the laptop looking at the unwanted future without my male genitals. The document on the desk was held together by a single paperclip. This was my chance.

I sidled up to the desk. The three ladies spun round. "What are you doing?" Elizabeth said.

"Since I have no choice in the matter, I thought I'd accept my fate and see what you plan to do to me."

Clara looked surprised, Dr Lopez uninterested and Elisabeth pleased. "Good that's better. Good girl."

She turned back to the screen and pointed out to me how pretty my new vagina was going to be. A big thick labia that would stand out in tight panties and bikinis. It would also allow me to wear a tampon, she told me. To feel like a proper girl.

As they discussed my proposed operation,

my right hand went out to the document. I kept my eyes firmly on the screen while Elizabeth waxed on about how wonderful it will be for me to have a vagina. My fingers curled around the clip. I put a long fingernail under it and pulled. The papers moved with the clip. I froze. No one noticed. I held the document down with my thumb and pushed the clip with a finger. It slid a little.

The ladies were finishing their discussion, I had to move fast. I took a chance and pushed. The clip slid off and onto the table. I palmed it.

Chapter 23 – Pegged and spanked

Clara was reading on the hotel bed and complaining about being my babysitter. Elizabeth's loyal servant wasn't happy about spending time guarding me. Elizabeth was back in her room next door relaxing. I had two days to make my escape. It wasn't much of a plan in truth: unpick the locks on my shoes and run for it. I didn't know the city of Sao Paulo or have anywhere to go; I had no money either.

I sat on my wide bed and gazed outside. Grey skies threatened rain. A cacophony of noise flowed through the single-glazed windows. Unseen dogs barked, car horns blared, people shouted. London was noisy but this was like a wall of sound.

The hotel room was vast; we both had our own king-sized bed. I had hidden the paperclip inside a bible in the bedside table drawer. I had put the clip between the pages and placed the bible back in the drawer. I was confident Clara would never look there.

Later that afternoon, Clara went to the bathroom again. The bathroom fan came on automatically. The noise was my cover. Great.

I retrieved the paperclip and inserted the straightened end into the tiny lock on my high heels. I twisted it with my fingers and manipulated the lock open without difficulty. I clipped the lock back and hid the clip between the pages again. I had a way to remove my high-heeled shoes. As I replaced the clip, I noticed Clara had left her flat shoes on the floor by her bed. They looked a similar size to my feet. They would be perfect for my getaway. I padded over and slipped a foot in. Maybe a half size too small but they would do. Flushing water and a running tap told me Clara was about to return. It had all come together. My great escape plan was on. Sometimes the best plans are the simple ones.

Once Clara went to have a shower later that evening, I would unpick the padlocks on my heels. I'd remove them, put on Clara's flat shoes and make a run for it. I decided I would find the Embassy and ask for them to help me to get home. That was the plan. Simple is best.

Clara was tall, well built and stronger than me, especially now I had slimmed down and my muscles atrophied. Overpowering her was not an option so my plan to run was the only answer.

Clara came out of the bathroom, her eyes half-closed, her face bored. She wandered around the room, looked out of the window then slumped on the bed. She sat up as if a thought had come into her head. It had.

She looked in my general direction. "I might as well have a bit of fun while I'm waiting."

That didn't sound good.

"Take your clothes off, Patty."

This wasn't good.

Her eyes bore down on me. I removed my skirt and top and unhooked my bra. I stood dressed only in high heels. She pulled me over her knee and spanked me. I yelped, asking what I'd done.

"Nothing," she said.

She was killing time by having fun at my

expense. Having fun for her was punishing me. Stinging slaps rained on my bare bum cheeks. I gritted my teeth. It wouldn't be long now. I had my plan. I allowed her slaps to wash over me. In an odd way, they were stimulating.

She pushed me off her legs and I slipped onto the floor. The hard brown carpet burned my skin. Clara hadn't finished with me. She pulled me up and pushed me down onto my bed face down. She pulled my legs wide apart.

"Stay there, don't move."

Her heavy footsteps padded away and returned. Her weight pushed the bed down as she loomed behind me. Something hard pushed against my bum hole then entered after a moment of resistance. The strap-on filled me.

She hadn't bothered with gel but it slid in as I

allowed my muscles to loosen against her penetration. She was too strong for me, I had to surrender and try to enjoy it. I pretended it was Elena pegging me. Clara's weight fell on me and her false cock went into the hilt. The strap slapped on my skin. She withdrew it. A moment later, she drove it in.

I bit against the bed cover. I'd grown to enjoy Elena pegging me. I wasn't about to give Clara the indication I wanted her to do what she was doing to me. I would have preferred it with the love Elena gave me. Elena wasn't here, nor would she be. I imagined it was her anyway, that it was her behind me, penetrating me.

Clara took it all the way out, teasing me then ramming it back inside me with force. I allowed my anus to surrender, to search for enjoyment in what was happening to me. I thought of the enjoyment I'd found when it had been Elena.

Elena thrust her false cock hard against the inside of my anus. There was a tingling pleasure. The relaxation helped and I allowed her to thrust at me, offering no resistance. I raised my bum to facilitate her pushes. I had a pang of guilt at Clara taking me but it was Elena in my mind. I had no choice.

Waves of strange pleasure flowed through me as she thrust and withdrew. My submission heightened my sexual fulfilment. She was rougher than Elena but in a different way. It was exciting, stimulating and gratifying to be taken by someone who was doing this as a power kick. I craved her power over me as a tide of gratification engulfed my mind. I forgot all about

Elena in the moments of pleasure.

Clara stopped and pulled me over and made me sit on the edge of the bed. She laid my penis on the side table. I froze thinking of the paperclip inside the drawer, a major part of my escape plan was inches away. I looked away not wanting to give any clues. She looked around for something in the room. Her eyes fell on her shoes. She grasped one and lifted it above her head. She slammed it down on my penis. I jumped and squealed like a banshee. She giggled like a maniac and slammed my penis again with the sole of her shoe.

She pulled me up and slipped her shoe on. She kicked a knee into my groin and I doubled up. Pain swamped my stomach. She laughed one more time then sat on the bed, seemingly satiated.

"I'm going for a shower after that workout. Get dressed, Patty."

My penis smarted, my bum was sore, but this was my chance. I had to clear my head. Clara looked at me for a moment and disappeared into the bathroom. The fan came on and I heard the shower water gushing.

I dressed quickly, putting on a plain dress. I retrieved the paperclip and unlocked the padlocks on my heels. I threw them to one side and squeezed into Clara's flat shoes. I picked up my small empty suitcase and stuffed some clothing in it without folding anything. This was the moment.

I went out the room door and closed it softly behind me. I was in the corridor. I looked both ways and I made for the lift and pressed the call button. I had pins and needles in my arms and sweaty palms. My eyes remained fixed on my hotel room door. The lift was two floors above me. It stopped above my floor. I glared at the indicator light above the lift doors. The click of a door in the corridor behind me made me jump. My stomach swirled as I looked in the direction of the noise. An elderly lady left her room two doors from my room. I breathed out.

The lift pinged and I jumped again. I was on edge. The lift doors slid open and I kept my eyes on the room door as I entered. A man stood at the back in the hotel uniform. The lift doors slid shut and we descended. I nodded at the man with a hotel name tag: Jorge Santos. He wasn't looking at my face, his eyes were fixed on my huge chest, bulging tight against my neat fitting low-cut dress.

The lift jolted to a halt on the ground floor. The doors opened. I faced Elizabeth.

Chapter 24 - Break out

We stared at each other for what seemed like minutes. It was only a second or two. Jorge Santos pushed past, impatient and busy. It broke us from our frozen state. We both went to move towards each other. I took a deep breath and pushed at Elizabeth with all my power. She hadn't expected that and lost her balance. She fell backwards and into a large green plant in a large terracotta pot. She lay splayed, legs out and plant leaves around her shocked face.

I took an instant to enjoy the scene. I picked up my case and ran towards the door. Two security guards stood by the door. Their legs were splayed apart like gunslingers, thumbs tucked into wide belts. Black revolver handles protruded from brown leather holsters. They were there to ensure no one undesirable entered the expensive hotel and disturbed the wealthy clientele. They had been looking outwards but turned to see what the commotion was at the lift. I looked back one more time at the prone dazed Elizabeth.

I'd wanted to continue my assault as months of frustration boiled over. Despite seething with rage, escape was the best way to defeat her. I needed to get away before she recovered though. Revenge would be my escape. The security men looked at me in stunned disbelief. The commotion they'd trained for was coming from inside not outside.

One recovered from the initial surprise and walked towards me. He put an arm out, blocking my way. Around me, the lobby area was full of people watching the scene. It was as if I was in a strange play in a weird theatre.

The guard hissed something at me in Portuguese. I didn't understand; it wasn't friendly. His open palm was inches from my face.

I looked behind, Elizabeth was struggling to get out of the plant pot. Two men were helping her. The guard grabbed my arm.

"What is going on?" he asked in a heavily accented English.

"It's nothing, a girly argument," I said. "I'm sorry, she'll pay for any damage." I pointed at Elizabeth still attempting to find her feet.

A ping sounded from the second lift and the doors opened. Clara stepped out. She had a towel wrapped around her body and a smaller one around her head. Water dripped onto the carpet around her. "Stop her," she cried out, pointing directly at me.

The guard tensed. The crowd gawped, watching the events unfold. Things were hotting up. The crowd parted and a tall gentleman in a well-fitted suit passed through. I didn't know what to do. I looked past the security man holding my arm and to the street outside. I smelled freedom. So near yet still out of reach. I flinched, ready to run. The security guard moved across to block my path, his hand dropped away to touch his holstered revolver.

The suited gentleman approached. He had a silver rectangular name tag on his left chest: *Gerente do Hotel Sr D. Oliveira*. Beneath in smaller letters in English, *Hotel Manager*.

Elizabeth had got up and pushed through the spectators. She glanced at Clara who had moved towards me too.

"What is going on here?" Sr Oliveira asked in an almost perfect US accent.

"I was going for a walk," I said.

"She's trying to escape," Clara pointed at me with an accusing finger.

Sr Oliveira's eyebrows knitted. "Escape from what exactly, madam?"

Clara's mouth opened and closed. She had no answer.

Elizabeth came closer and took my arm. "This is no more than a silly little argument." She stared at the manager's name tag and smiled. "Mr Oliveira. I'm sure if Patty came back to her room with me, we could sort things out between us. No need for you to be involved. I'm sorry for the disturbance, Mr Oliveira."

"That would seem to be a very good idea, Ms Remington." The manager said.

"I will, of course, pay for any damage and compensate your hotel for the disturbance." Elizabeth dug her fingers into my arm.

I shook them away as Sr Oliveira spoke to the closest security guard. "Escort the ladies back to their rooms, would you please, Joao? "

"Sim Senhor, *yes sir*," the guard answered.

The guard took my arm and Clara relaxed. Elizabeth's face grinned in satisfaction. I was trapped and desperate, it seemed as if my escape plan had failed. My heart pounded fiercely against my chest. I made to walk towards the door but the security guard's hand tightened around my arm. I looked past him towards the street outside. Our party moved towards the lift and the spectators move apart, the action finished.

"Patricia, Patricia. There you are." A woman's voice called out. It was familiar. An English accent.

Someone pushed past the security guard and stood in our way. Elena. My mouth dropped open.

She spoke in rapid fluent Portuguese to Sr Oliveira. His face broke into a smile. What was Elena doing here? How did she speak Brazilian Portuguese?

She pushed the security guard's hand away and took my hand. She led me out of the hotel and into the street. Elizabeth and Clara looked on in stunned disbelief, unmoving. The hotel bell boy in the street hailed a taxi immediately and Elena bundled me in.

I sat in shock. What on Earth had just happened?

Chapter 25 - Domesticated

I put the last plate in the dishwasher and closed the door. It clicks into place and I push the wash button. It groans into life as if in complaint about the effort it will be expending.

I've almost finished working for the evening. I go to the dining room; my calves ache as my muscles have not yet become used to the shorter heels. Elena thought three inches heels were more appropriate. There's no lock on these shoes, there's no need. I wear them with pleasure.

My chest is lighter as I glide through the house. Elena paid for me to undergo breast reduction, she said 40C boobs are much more practical than what I had before. They're still a little sore after the surgery, but I'm happy. They are still very large but not grotesque like before.

"Is there anything else you require, Madam?" I curtsy as I enter the room, holding my mid-thigh length pink housemaid's dress out wide on either side as I dip. I mean this curtsey with respect not because I'm ordered to.

Elena thinks it proper I wear a maid's outfit when serving dinner and when cleaning for her. I have no objection and I like the feel of the satin. I will do anything she asks with pleasure.

"That will be all for tonight, Patty. You may come and sit down with us." Elena pointed to her feet. Her two friends sat on either side of her, fighting smirks. I don't mind.

I curtsey again and untie the little white apron. I lay it over the back of a chair. "Thank you, Madam."

I sit at her feet, my love for her hurts. I fidget as I make myself comfortable, allowing my pink silicone cock cage to settle comfortably under my clothing. Elena doesn't want me as a man so my penis is never going to enter her. She insists it's locked away and out of the way. I never grumble about this, of course not. If that's what Elena wants, it works for me.

Oddly, I rather like wearing it for her. It's much better than the metal tube Elizabeth had put me in and exposed the end of my penis. I shuddered at the thought of the little face Clara used to draw on the end.

My desperation to cum makes me more pliable. I love being pliable for Elena. The edge I feel in rarely cumming leaves me in a permanent state of excitement and submission. She controls the rare times when he permits my ejaculation. I am eternally grateful when she allows my sexual release.

We have a loving sex life. I give her oral and she takes me with her strap-on. She's a gentle lover and started with a small dildo cock. She has gradually increased the size. I'm stretching inside as she increases the size.

When she allows my relief around every two or three months, I have to masturbate in front of her. Sometimes, she masturbates me. This is a special treat. She wears kitchen gloves as she doesn't like my mess on her skin. She gets no sexual excitement from me cumming, she does it to relieve me and because it appears to amuse her.

She's said she wants to introduce me to other sissies and they can become my girlfriends. She says she wants to watch us love each other. This sounds awful but I'll do anything for her. I'm not sure why the idea makes me hard inside my cage.

Elena chats to the two female friends she's invited for dinner. Both glance at me, still unable to register what they are seeing. Elena explained she had thought it best to introduce me as soon as possible so they were able to become accustomed to our relationship. Relationship. I roll the word around my mind and I like it.

As the three friends chat, I think back to that time when Elena had appeared in the Brazilian hotel lobby. Elena had explained, on the way to Sao Paulo airport, she'd found out I'd gone to Brazil from the pub manager, Suzie. Elena had gone there to find out what was going on after she'd heard the air hostess telling me to switch off the phone when I'd called her.

Suzie had told Elena I was to have my penis removed and a proper vagina made. Elizabeth hadn't thought to tell Suzie it was a secret as she didn't expect anyone to care about me. From there, Elena paid a private investigator to track us to Sao Paulo and to find me.

I am a full-time housewife to Elena. Yesterday she told me she would like to get married. I was ecstatic. As I think about this at her feet, she shows me an IPad tablet image of a wedding dress she had been discussing with her friends.

"Do you like this one, Patty?" It is for me.

It is white and flared out from the waist with

layers of white frilled petticoats. It is short for a wedding dress — mid-thigh. This is unusual for a wedding dress but I nod enthusiastically. Her two friends laugh at this. Elena explains she wants the dress altered so it's open at the front to show my cock cage. She says she wants to attach a leash to it and hold it during the ceremony.

She's still searching for a minister who will perform a service like this, but she said it's necessary. I agree despite my reservations about being exposed in front of a congregation.

I'll need a divorce from Elizabeth, I don't expect that to pose a problem. Elena has it all in hand, I trust her.

Elena promises a trip to the shopping centre tomorrow. Although she has purchased new clothing for me, she wants to replenish my wardrobe with what she considers more appropriate clothing. No more micro skirts that don't cover me, although she wants to see me in mini skirts and little dresses.

She's changed my hair colour to a more natural light brown from the platinum blond of before. Elena likes it long and feminine though, so that's not changed.

I don't have to worry about financial matters or complicated issues. Elena takes care of everything. She told me not to worry my pretty little head about things. It's nice to be told I'm pretty. Elena likes me to look good for her. I make sure when she comes home from work, I look pretty for her and the home is spotless. I change out of my working maid's dress and into a pretty dress for her after finishing my housework. I do my hair and put on fresh lipstick and freshen up my makeup.

Elena always texts to say she's on her way home. I wait at the front door for her, curtsey when she comes in and take her jacket and bag. She has even bought me a mobile phone.

I've started going to the nail bar alone to have my nails done and the hairdresser every week. Elena gives me a small housekeeping allowance for this and to get things for the home when necessary. She doesn't give me much housekeeping money, enough for a few things. I'm only a silly girly.

She has a couple of pet names for me: Princess, sometimes Pretty Princess. She also calls me petal, flower, girly or sissy. I die with love when she says those names to me.

It's hard to remember my previous life as a man. The itinerant musician who wasted his life and never respected women; the narcissistic man who always put himself first. I'm not that person any more. I now put someone else first: Elena.

And I am feminized and pretty.

THE END

Dear Reader,

I hope you enjoyed the concluding book in the three-part series 'Petticoated and Pretty'.

Please could you spare a moment to share your thoughts on Petticoated and Pretty 3 by posting a quick review.

Thank you so much for reading my stories

Alexa Martínez (aka Lady Alexa)

xxx

PS, why not drop me a line to share your thoughts on my books?
ladyalexa@mail.com

Printed in Great Britain
by Amazon

83242073R00166